Diving Home

Stories of Diving Deep and Finding Home

Catee Ryan

Editors: Lara Tupper http://www.laratupper.com
        Robin Ryan Robinryan14@gmail.com
        Lee Miller

Illustrations: Jennifer C. Smith
jensmithdesign@earthlink.net
All Rights Reserved

Photographer: Kelly Woodrum

ISBN-10: 0692896414
ISBN-13: 978-0692896419

Catee Ryan
Box 836
Cathedral City, CA
92235

$12.99

to dad and mom

The Collection

Maine

Morning Swims

Emma sits at the old, scarred wooden table in her mother's kitchen. A stack of cleaning rags that her mother cut into neat squares from old towels sit on the table. When Emma picks up the towel-squares she is startled from her reverie by the ping of metal hitting metal. She sees something round resting next to the old milk can turned umbrella holder. She puts down the cleaning rags and picks up the coin and sees a swimmer engraved on it. On the other side, Emma reads 1950 Olympic Trials, First Place. She stares at the medallion in her hand. Could this have belonged to her mother? And if it had, why didn't her mother tell her she'd been in the Olympic Trials?

Emma cries as she rests her head on the old towels. *Waste not, want not.* That's what her mother used to say. Emma is grateful for these old, faded, colorful towel-squares that catch her tears and bring back memories.

As she sits at the kitchen table holding the medallion and drinking peppermint tea that was her mother's favorite, Emma now understands why, every morning, her mother went to the misty cold water and made her way into the lake. Emma never understood this before. She only watched as her mother silently put on one of her many Speedo swimsuits, changing from red to blue to green and then, one day, yellow. Yellow, only once. The towels changed too, stripes and polka dots-red and white, green and white, pink and orange, and the two-tone blue. Emma liked the pink and orange towel the best.

Emma gets undressed and goes to the wall of suits hanging on pegs by the back door. She picks the yellow Speedo and realizes it isn't too late to honor her mother. She smiles as she hits the cold steamy water and begins to swim the three-mile loop around the lake. With every stroke she takes, she feels her mother's presence.

Emma wishes that just one time she had gone with her mother into the water, and they had swum together in the beautiful silence of another morning.

The Polka-Dotted Purse

Emma sits at her mother's kitchen table after finding a letter her mother had written but never sent. Wanting to see her mother's handwriting one more time, she opens the letter and begins to read.

Dear Marsha,

I write to you because I found the leather polka-dotted purse you gave me when I was doing a major spring cleaning. I raved about it the first time you showed it to me. I imagine lots of people expressed that same sentiment over the years. When you gave it to me you told me it had been your mother's, your grandmother's, and your great grandmother's, that the purse was important in your maternal lineage. When I asked you, why me, you said, you didn't know. After a long silence, you walked out.

That was the end of our relationship. I lost you and my best friend, Dorothy. I was hurt and angry for a long time. I had no idea how to make peace with your dismissal. I did not know how to forgive you, not for your sake, but for mine. My calls went unanswered and you did not respond to my letters. Eventually I stopped trying. I felt like you paid me off with the purse because you felt guilty about sleeping with Dorothy. I didn't think you liked her that much. I thought you wanted to be free of me and you couldn't end our relationship any other way. I was wrong. You and Dorothy were together for forty years. I saw her obituary in the paper. I thought about attending her funeral, but I didn't.

So, Marsha, I wrote a story about the polka-dotted purse. I included pictures and the cobbler's copious notes.

The story goes that after your great grandmother, Harriet Marie Belcher, finished her walk along the coast, she wandered around Ogunquit and discovered a shoe repair shop. Upon entering it, she heard the tinkling bells that let the owner know a customer had arrived and saw the polka-dotted purse sitting on the counter. She'd never seen anything like it before and was immediately drawn to it.

When the cobbler came out in his old, cracked, brown leather apron and saw Harriet admiring the purse, he was in a quandary. He had forgotten to put the purse in the back room and could tell she wanted it. He had promised himself that if someone wanted to buy it, he would make sure he told them the purse's history.

The cobbler took off his gold wire-rim glasses and cleaned them. He told Harriet that ten years ago Leticia Maxwell Brown brought him this soft, supple, smooth Italian leather that he'd never seen the likes of before and asked him to design and make her a purse. He told Harriet he'd seen a lot of leather in his day, but none as nice as this. It was easy to work with, and its feel and smell were intoxicating. He was embarrassed about his love for the leather, but Harriet who was quiet and attentive as she listened to the cobbler, asked him to continue on with the story as she stroked the leather purse. She loved his passion and admired the creative mastery of the purse. It was a work of art.

He told her that Leticia disappeared before he finished making her purse. He read about her disappearance in the paper. Her partner, Brita Ann McClinton, went to the police and filed a missing person's report. The police thought there might be foul play. They discovered the lesbian-love-affair of Leticia Maxwell Brown and Brita Ann McClinton. The cobbler liked Leticia and didn't care about her lifestyle or the town gossip. He cared about making her a purse she loved. Leticia insisted upon paying in advance for the purse. He wondered about that at the time. And then she went missing.

Harriet told him she vaguely remembered reading about that missing person case in the weekly Belfast News. The cobbler nodded and showed Harriet a scrapbook where he kept all the newspaper articles about the case as well as his designs and measurements for the purse, and its tag, #27, as if the purse needed a tag. But the cobbler was a man of order and he did his business by the book.

The cobbler told Harriet that he had called and sent letters to Brita every year for the past ten years, but she never responded. He put ads in the classified section of the local paper, the NY Times, and the Boston Globe. He put his name, Samuel Watkins, Village Cobbler, his address, and his phone number. No one had come to claim the purse. He had numerous offers for the purse, but it never felt right to sell it. He kept hoping that one day Leticia would show up and claim her purse. He mulled over how long he should hold onto the purse, and had just the day before talked to his wife about it. She told him that after ten years, he could sell the purse.

Over peppermint tea Samuel continued telling Harriet the purse's history. Then he sold her the purse and gave her the scrapbook. He insisted they belonged together.

So Marsha, soon after I got my story published, the grand-niece of Leticia Maxwell Brown showed up on my doorstep. I invited her in and we had a conversation over peppermint tea. And even though you and I have not spoken in years, I am writing to tell you that Leticia Maxwell Brown's niece wants to meet you. I gave her your contact information. I know how important the purse's story is to you and your maternal lineage.
I hope you're well,
Ester

Emma sits quietly at the kitchen table. She stares at the box addressed to Marsha Malone. She will send the purse and the letter that her mother wrote to Marsha or maybe she will go to Castine and deliver the package in person. *Aah mom, you are full of secrets. I wish we could talk. I miss you terribly.*

A Glass Mermaid

What has surfaced today in our harbor? I'm on shore and see objects moving together in a large mass. I don't know what they are. I would like them to be colored-glass fishing balls. When they come closer I see they are misshapen chunks of colored styrofoam that look like some creature has taken a bite out of them. The harbor is filled with these floating pieces. I wonder where they came from. The tide and winds from last night's storm must have brought these colored chunks to our harbor. It rained hard last night and the wind howled. Things got ravaged.

Today the water is still and the autumn sky is a beautiful blue, the calm after the storm. In some odd way the colors bobbing up and down and pushing into each other are beautiful. A seagull lands on one of the pieces and looks surprised when it is not edible. It does look good enough to eat.

At first I'm alone. A part of me wants to dive in and swim with these chunks. Fear holds me back. I'm riveted by these styrofoam pieces. I don't know why I'm drawn to them. It doesn't really matter why. Will I go in and swim with them? The styrofoam drifts closer to shore.

I see a young woman looking at the craggy floating pieces. She throws rocks at them as she moves closer to where I'm standing. I don't move. I recognize the young woman. It's SaraLouise, a seventeen-year old whose picture I recently saw in our local paper, the Castine Patriot. She won a kayaking race two weekends ago. She's a good looking, popular kid. Yet, here she is alone on a Sunday morning. She sees me and waves. I wave back. As she approaches, the wind picks up and the styrofoam dances in the light. The chunks collide.

She asks, "What do you make of this?"
I tell her, "I don't know. I've never seen anything like it."
Then a strange thing happens.
She says, "I really want to swim with the chunks."
I turn to her. "Me too, but I'm afraid."
She looks at me, an older woman, alone on the beach. She knows who I am. I used to teach at the primary school and I've lived in this town for decades. Four years ago, Dorothy, my partner of

forty years, died. SaraLouise must have come to her memorial service. It seems like the whole town came that day.

"Hi, SaraLouise," I say.

"Hello, Miss Malone. I haven't see you since Dorothy's service."

"I thought you might have been there," I say with a sigh. "I retired five years ago."

"Yes," she says. "Dorothy had cancer, and it was a long slow unveiling."

I am struck with SaraLouise's use of the word *unveiling*, because that is precisely what it was, a long slow process where Dorothy's true essence became revealed. She became total light and love, even with all her pain. Her cancer ate her up, yet she was not angry at the end. Only I was angry at the end.

SaraLouise and I are quiet as we look out at the densely packed, constantly changing mass of floating chunks. We look at each other, and with a slight nod, we have agreed to go into the water. At first we have to maneuver our way through the colored chunks. My lower body feels cold, and soon, I will be numb. The water is always cold here in Maine, no matter what time of year it is. The cold sucks the life right out of you. SaraLouise and I know this. I imagine she can last longer than me. I remind myself this is not an endurance contest.

I see an opening and begin to swim. Isn't it often like this? An opening appears, and you take it, or you don't. I took it with Dorothy. She would have cheered me on from the shore, while I went in to explore the chunks. She never liked cold water. I went in many times while she watched, walked on the beach, or sat and painted.

SaraLouise calls to me. She's ahead. I swim nine swift strokes to reach her and see her pointing at a sunken boat. My heart surges. I pray to God no one is dead. Questions come. How long has the boat been here? Is the styrofoam from this boat? It doesn't seem big enough to hold all these chunks.

SaraLouise is excited. She's diving under, swimming, coming up for air, and then going back down again. I do the same, although my stamina is less. Aah, to be seventeen and a girl with all that boundless energy pumping through her veins.

I do not see any dead bodies. I feel relieved.

When SaraLouise surfaces after the fourth or fifth time, she says, "There's a statue. I think it's a glass mermaid."

I look at her with my mouth open, not comprehending. I can't quite take in what she's saying. I can understand the words, but I'm finding it hard to believe. A glass mermaid? SaraLouise signals me, and we both dive down. I see the mermaid, a bit angled, but upright. I look into her eyes and see a sultry expression on her face with just a hint of a smile. The mermaid exudes sexual energy. I like her. Bonnie. That's the name that comes to me, and then the song. *My Bonnie lies over the ocean. My Bonnie lies over the sea. My Bonnie lies over the ocean. Please bring back my Bonnie to me.*

I'm out of air, so I surface.

SaraLouise stares at me and says, "You were down there a long time. Are you okay?"

I nod yes, but don't say anything.

SaraLouise must see something in my face.

"The statue is beautiful," I say. Then I add, "She's come to us."

She looks at me, nods, and says, "I imagine the styrofoam was protecting her."

"Yes," I say.

We've moved into practicality now.

"The statue looks heavy. I can't move it," she says. "I'm going to get my Dad, and see if he'll bring out the lobster boat so we can bring it up with the winch."

I hear myself say, "Bonnie."

She looks at me for a moment. A flicker of a smile crosses her face. We break into song. *My Bonnie lies over the ocean...* I'm laughing and crying. SaraLouise's alto voice is rich and strong. For a minute I forget she's seventeen.

"It's getting cold. Thirty minutes is way up, and we shouldn't lose any more of our body heat," SaraLouise says.

The practicality of this young woman doesn't surprise me. She's a Mainer and knows that cold can kill you. We make our way back through the narrow styrofoam passageway.

When we reach the shore, she says, "I'm going to get my Dad."

I tell her, "I need to go home and jump in the hot shower."

It is more than the cold that I need to contend with. It is the mermaid's expression, and how I feel as though I've been summoned. I'm being asked to do something and I don't know what that is. Yet I know I want to be up for the challenge, because that's what it feels like, a challenge.

Before SaraLouise and I part she asks me if I need her to walk me home. The consideration of this young woman! I like her.

"No," I say with sincerity. "I'll be fine. How about we meet in an hour?"

She agrees.

"My Dad will be up for this," she says.

"Yes," I say, "I'm up for it myself."

"Bonnie," she says.

"Bonnie," I say back.

Then we turn our separate ways. I walk swiftly. SaraLouise runs. I feel alive for the first time since Dorothy died. As I walk back to my house I think about the boat, its crew, and passengers. I'm glad I didn't see any dead bodies; only *Bonnie,* this glass beauty rising out of the ruin, like the phoenix who rises from the ashes.

I've always been fascinated by deterioration. I like to watch things fall apart, disintegrate, and change into something new. Again, questions float through my mind. Who makes large glass mermaid sculptures? Will *Bonnie* change our small Maine village? Will SaraLouise and I be bound together by this discovery?

When I get home I jump in the shower, grab something to eat, and head back to the beach to meet SaraLouise and her dad. They have a plan for bringing up the glass mermaid. I sit on the boat and watch as *Bonnie* surfaces. SaraLouise's dad smiles at me. SaraLouise is in the water. This time she is in a full-body wetsuit. When she gives her father a thumbs up, her dad cranks the winch and bit by bit Bonnie surfaces. The statue is at least five feet tall and looks like a beautiful, young adult woman. Her face is eerily human, her mouth is open, and she looks like she is talking. I wonder what she would say if she could speak. The statue is mysterious, haunting, and stunningly majestic.

A crowd has gathered on the beach. The village is all in a flutter about this glass mermaid. I hear a lot of speculation about where she came from and how she ended up here. Everyone has a story.

At the emergency town meeting the next day SaraLouise and I talk about finding the mermaid statue. The community agrees to name the statue Bonnie and discusses where to install her. Some people want her in the town square while others think her place should be at the entrance to the harbor. Everyone has an opinion, and everyone's voice is heard. Most of the children want Bonnie in town. When it's time to vote, the town square advocates have more support and Bonnie is installed there.

With Bonnie's arrival I feel closer to people in the village. I'm involved in the community again. I've started a writing group at the library that SaraLouise comes to every week. She and I are talking about writing a children's book. I still miss Dorothy terribly, but I no longer feel so alone. Dorothy would have loved the mermaid and I know she would have drawn and painted many pictures of her. I feel Dorothy's spirit with me all the time now. I sing Bonnie's praises every day.

The Block Party

At the block party my interest in Jill wanes with every beer she consumes. I see her flirt with the new tenant, Brandon, whose dick immediately gets hard when she drapes herself around him. Part of him likes her attention, but I see confusion in his eyes. When he looks around no one is giving him approval. No one is paying any attention to him or Jill, except me.

Everyone here knows Jill and they stopped playing her game years ago, but Brandon's new. I watch Paul peel Jill off Brandon's thin shoulder. Brandon looks haunted. I think he might be embarrassed at being in this odd predicament-his first block party, a beautiful sexy woman coming onto him, and then Paul's interference.

Jill doesn't like Paul taking Brandon away from her. She calls him a fucking asshole. Paul expertly takes Jill's arm and leads her to the wooden bench in our beautiful community garden filled with daffodils and tulips. I hope Jill doesn't step on the flowers. Surprisingly, she stays on the slate path. Brandon watches them go and I see his dick get small. I remember Jill coming on to me when I was new, and Alicia talking to me while Paul led Jill away. I didn't listen to Alicia. I went home with Jill, and we fucked all night. I couldn't get enough of her. In the morning Jill was very cool towards me and asked me what I was doing in her house. It was clear she didn't remember our incredible sex, and it was also clear she wanted me gone.

It took me a long time to get Jill out of my system. I had difficulty moving on. Strange. We only had sex that one night, but Jill's sexual freedom opened up a raw, vulnerable place in myself that I didn't know how to shut down. I felt so alive the night I'd been with her. When I had sex with other women, I found myself comparing them to Jill. It was never as good. I didn't understand what happened. Eventually I talked to Alicia because I couldn't get Jill off my mind. She told me the history of Jill's progressing alcoholism and how everyone in the neighborhood had been involved with her. After that conversation I started therapy with Marcy McDougal. I got a whole lot more than I bargained for.

I talked about forbidden sex that I liked and wanted with my step-father, Joe. I hadn't told anyone about my relationship with Joe until I started seeing Marcy. I covered up and buried my feelings for ten years. Sex with Jill tripped me back into that loss.

"What am I supposed to do?" That's the question I asked Marcy McDougal nearly every session for the year I was in therapy. "My mother worked five nights a week. She left at 10:30 p.m. I'd get home from waitressing around midnight and check-in with Joe. He'd be in bed asleep. I'd touch his cheek and say, *Joe, I'm home.*

He'd open one eye and say, *Okay, Dawn. Glad you're home safe.*

Sometimes he had no covers on, and I'd see his amazing body. He slept naked, and as the summer progressed I began to see him get hard when I woke him. At first I was scared by that, but things changed the day I turned eighteen. We had a big birthday bash with family and friends who came over and stayed until my mother left for work. Afterwards, Joe and I were in the kitchen cleaning up. I was aware of Joe looking at me and I looked right back at him with the same intensity. When our shoulders touched I felt electricity shooting through me. He felt it too. He put the platter into the dishwasher, put the soap in, and punched the button.

When he turned to me, I saw a look I'd never seen in him before. I'd seen that look between couples in the movies, between heterosexual couples, and between Emma and Rikki when they walked arm in arm, kissed, and rubbed up against each other when they thought no one was looking. I'd never felt it myself or had anyone express it towards me. Joe stood there. I stood there. Then he put his mouth on mine and pushed his tongue hard into my mouth, and my body moved directly into his. I wanted him. He wanted me. He carried me to my bed and we made love all night long. I couldn't get enough, it's like I was starving. Later he told me he'd wanted to take me on the kitchen table but knew I was a virgin and he didn't want that to be my first sexual experience. We never made love in their bed. I respected him for that as well as for waiting until I was eighteen. The energy between us was palpable. We had difficulty keeping our hands off each other. I don't know how my mother didn't see it.

That was the year I came alive. Joe was a good lover. I was open. My history teacher asked me what was going on. I feigned

---

knowing what she was talking about. She didn't know who, but she knew. Five nights a week Joe and I slept together. We were the couple. My mother was peripheral. Joe told me they weren't having sex anymore and that he wanted to leave her. We talked about him going with me to wherever I went to college.

I said, *Yes.* We made our escape plan.

In late May, just before graduation, everything changed. I came home from school and saw a police car outside my house. When I went in my mother was sitting quietly at the kitchen table with a cigarette and a cup of coffee. She had her favorite mug that had red and white stripes and reminded me of a candy-cane. Printed on it was *Santa Claus Lives.* The police officer had a cup of coffee, too, in the dark blue cup with sparkly silver stars all over it. Joe's cup. *Why would my mother give the police officer Joe's cup?* I couldn't understand it. My mother had a vacant look on her face and was staring out the window. When she told me to sit down, she did not look me in the eyes. I felt the tug of resistance, but I sat.

She looked at the police officer and nodded. He said, *Joe was in an accident. He died on the way to the hospital. I'm sorry.*

I didn't say anything at first. I just sat there. Then I squeaked out, *How?*

Head on collision, drunk driver.

My whole world crumbled that day. The summer was a blur. In his will, Joe left me the cabin on Lake Anasagunticook in Maine and his family's thousand acres in Virginia. He paid my college tuition and put additional money in a trust. He paid off my mother's house. She was furious that I got more than her, but there was nothing she could do. Joe took care of me, yet I was left with so much sadness and unexpressed grief.

During my sessions with Marcy I cried and raged and told her I was sick of watching the succession of men and women go up against Jill at the block parties. I talked about seeing Brandon deflate when Paul led Jill away at that last block party. Remembering sex with Jill pushed me over some line. I felt all that old grief and could not tamp it down anymore. In therapy I got clear that I had a choice. I could stay in my neighborhood or I could leave. If I stayed I would have to set boundaries. I wasn't ready to set boundaries, so I put my house up for sale. It sold in three days.

I've been living at Joe's cabin on Lake Anasagunticook ever since. At first I lived on my inheritance. Then I got a job at the post office in the small town near the lake. I met Sami when I delivered a Christmas package to her house, which was across the lake from my place. I was leaving a big box on her porch when she drove up in her Subaru. What can I say? I was smitten from the beginning. She later told me she was too.

It's great to have a partner. We kayak back and forth between our houses and spend most nights together. Sometimes we sleep alone because we want to be in our own spaces. I love my house. I've cleaned it out and it feels like mine now. It holds a lot of history. Joe would like what I've done with it.

When I get the invitation to the Christmas block party, I do two things; I invite Sami to go with me and I schedule an appointment with Marcy McDougal. I've had monthly phone appointments with her since I moved to the lake. She's helped me with leaving the old neighborhood, settling into my new lake-life, and more recently, getting used to being a couple with Sami.

I've stayed in touch with most of my old neighbors. They tell me Jill has gone to rehab. I tell them about Sami. I know the old gang is happy for me. I'm excited to show off Sami, who I'm crazy in love with. I think it's the real deal this time. Sex is great and so is the trust and communication. We tell the truth, no holds barred.

Sometimes I find myself asking her, *What am I supposed to do?*

Sami laughs and says, *Really, Dawn! Am I Marcy McDougal?*

I laugh and grab her. I kiss her on the lips. We play like young cubs.

I say, *It's you and me, Sami-baby.*

The Holly G's

You said you were listening to The Holly G's sing *Darlin'
Your Life is Gonna Change* when your water broke, Mom. When I
was little, I never understood what you meant. I wondered if your
water breaking was like when I got sopping wet when a boy threw a
water balloon at me at my seventh birthday party.

As I got older I tried talking to you a bunch of times about
your water breaking, but you would never tell me. Even when I was
old enough to understand what you were talking about, Mom, we
never talked about it. Apparently, it wasn't a conversation you
wanted to have.

Another conversation we never had was who my father was
and why he didn't come to see me. You and Barbara played this off
too, Mom. I didn't like being different. I wanted a dad. Instead I had
two moms. Having two moms was fine, but I didn't like the no-dad
part. With you and Barbara so tight-lipped about the whole thing,
somewhere in middle school I gave up asking who my father was.

When you both died in that car crash a week before my
eighteenth birthday, I felt so alone. Children's Protective Services
didn't take me because Aunt Marsha and Aunt Dorothy took me in,
but they couldn't take on the responsibility for very long. Luckily
they didn't have to.

It's not that they didn't love me, they do. It's just that Aunt
Marsha couldn't be responsible for another person. She was teaching
at the primary school, still working with Iranian girls who had
escaped, and she had just learned that Dorothy had terminal cancer.
She baked a cake and threw a party for my eighteenth birthday. Now
that I was legally an adult I moved back to our house.

I was thrust into adulthood and spent many nights sitting in
your red leather chair, Mom, listening to the Holly G's while I went
through your file cabinets. I threw most of the stuff away, but in the
back of the small file cabinet I found a file labeled *Birth*. It was full

of pictures of you and Barbara, you pregnant with me, and pictures of me as a baby. I was surprised to find paperwork about my father, Morgan Green, and a picture of him as a young man. Looking at him was like looking at myself. There were letters from him asking to see me, wanting to share responsibility for me, and cancelled checks that showed he contributed financially to my upbringing. His last letter was written a couple of years before your accident. I found his phone number and called him. It was disconnected. Then I wrote a letter that I got back a few weeks later stamped with *No Forwarding Address*.

I talked to Aunt Marsha who was surprised you had a file on Morgan Green.

"He was a good guy, Sami."

"Then why did she keep him from me?"

"She was afraid if she gave an inch, she'd lose you, and Barbara didn't want him in their lives."

Aunt Marsha's never been shy about telling the truth. It would be easy for me to blame Barbara, but I don't. Clearly you had your reasons, Mom, for keeping Morgan out of my life.

By the time you and Barbara had been dead a couple of years, and I was in college and working full-time, I met Dawn. I was finding my way around my sexuality. I liked the sex with both men and women, but realized I liked talking with girls more. I followed in your footsteps, Mom. You would be proud. You'd like Dawn, Mom. We're thinking about living together.

Then The Holly G's announced they were doing a benefit concert for abused women in Boston. Dawn and I got tickets. She liked The G's, too. I put on one of your old hippie skirts, boots, and a shawl, and Dawn wore the standard black pants and white button-down shirt with an off-beat bright purple jacket with gold tassels. We were quite the couple, having a night out on the town. There were lots of single men in line, about an equal number of gay and straight couples, a lot of forty-something parents, and their twenty-something children who grew up listening to The G's.

While Dawn and I waited in line, she started nudging me. I got irritated by her poking my shoulder and saying *Sami* as I was having an intense conversation with an old friend.

"What?" I said and turned to her.

But I should have known Dawn wouldn't poke me without good reason. So the fire in my eyes tempered the minute I saw the expression on her face. She pointed. I turned. There he was, Morgan Green, an older version of the picture that I'd found in the birth file. He was in line with a woman who looked a hell of a lot like you, Mom. I stared. He must have felt my eyes on him because he turned at that moment and looked directly at me. His mouth went slack, and his eyes got large. He leaned in and said something to the woman. She turned and gazed at me. I saw her squeeze his elbow and push him lightly in his mid-back as though she was guiding him to me.

"Samantha?" I nodded. My eyes never left his face. Nobody called me Samantha, although it is the name on my birth certificate, and it is how I sign my checks.

"Morgan…Dad?"

He nodded to me just like I had nodded to him. I walked into his outstretched arms.

The Lament

Right from the start, you say to me, "Slow down, Alice. Getting quiet is the key."

I get angry at you because I think you're trying to control me, but later, I see you're actually wanting to help me. I'm spinning and gyrating with and without the drugs. At first they make me creative, but later, I can't focus. I can't get to the story. I can't make my point, and I desperately want to make my point.

And the point is…It can be so many things, Charlie. I don't know if I can successfully navigate the waters of my mind and the water in the lake. It's easy for me to dive in and swim breast stroke underwater to the raft. I like being with you, Charlie, and Billy and Su. I like swimming to the raft at sunset, passing a joint, and splashing my feet in the water. I like the four of us doing yoga and meditating together.

What happened, Charlie? I can't believe you're gone. They found your body in the river. They say you drowned. How can that be? I'll never understand it. You are the quintessential swimmer. You can swim under water without coming up for air for three minutes, easy. Maybe you got caught in the underwater growth, but Billy and I don't believe that. He's hurting, too. I haven't seen him lately, and we don't get high together anymore. He's working long hours at the mill, and I've got a live-in job taking care of Mrs. Carson, whose mind is going.

I've cleaned up my act, Charlie. You'd be proud of me. You might not even recognize me. I don't get loaded anymore. On my days off, I go to that deserted cabin we found on the lake. I want quiet. I need it. It's my new drug. You told me that quiet is the key, and if I'm still, I can find myself. You were right, Charlie. When I enter the dead zone, I'm immediately struck by the quiet. You told me I'd be awed, and I am. I listen with my new-found ability to listen, Charlie. I couldn't do this when I first met you. I was always moving.

I liked being your girlfriend, Charlie. I never said this to you. I'm sorry I couldn't tell you, but I couldn't see myself needing anyone.

Now I'm different. Mrs. Viola Carson, I like her, Charlie. She's got Alzheimer's and is like a quiet child. She and I get on. I take her out in the rowboat. I work my muscles rowing. We sit quietly in the middle of the lake and watch the loons dive for food, call to each other, and play. Watching the loons makes Viola happy. It makes me happy too, Charlie.

I'm working my way towards happiness, Charlie. I'm making my way through the dead zone to acceptance, that there's a life without you, that's worth living.

Clementine's Secret

Clementine works at Marlow's, a reputable Miami sex club. She's worked in sleazy clubs before, and they were like being in Hell, or at least what she imagines Hell to be. For the past ten years Clementine has been raising and supporting her daughter and herself by working in these clubs. She is good at fucking men and making them feel comfortable. She likes that men like her body. Truth be told, she likes the regular, on-going sex and orgasms. Most of the men like that she has orgasms.

The illusion that they are actually in a relationship is important to many of her clientele and these men pay to spend the night with her. She leaves the club at 4:30 a.m. sharp, so she can get home to her daughter by 6:30 a.m. All *her men* know about her daughter, and accept that she must leave to get home in time to get her daughter off to school.

Jorga, Marlow's owner, doesn't care how long the men stay because they pay by the hour. Her club is one of the few that allow men to stay extended hours. Jorga is grateful for Clementine's ability to be with men who have the desire for something more than sex, for some semblance of intimacy, where after sex there is cuddling and talking. Clementine likes the talking.

Sometimes she dresses up in different costumes, the milkmaid, the slut, the librarian. All the costumes and fantasies, hers and theirs, work. Some of the men are rough, but Clementine can handle rough. She likes their big hands and big penises. All *her men* want to be cared about. Sometimes their need for comfort is a bigger need than sex. Most of the men have wives and children. Clementine knows their names.

Although Clementine's customers know about her daughter, Colette, they do not know that Clementine grew up on a farm outside of Belfast, Maine and got pregnant after her parents' friend, Claude, raped her. Clementine hates to think of herself as a woman who's been raped.

She was seventeen when Claude first raped her. He tied her down and was in and out of every one of her orifices. He talked to her about how her body liked sex, would like it, and then at some point, she did like it. However, she did not like his cock being shoved in her mouth and his semen nearly choking her. She did like fucking and coming. She bled that first time. He'd been surprised and pleased that she was a virgin. It excited him.

Claude said, *I can't believe you haven't fucked your boyfriend. What's wrong with him? He hasn't tried to get in your pants?*

Clementine remained quiet as Claude spoke. He was right. She and her boyfriend, Connor, weren't having sex. She was rubbing her body on top of his until she came. Then she would suck him off. She did not want to get pregnant, and Connor did not want her to get pregnant either. They loved each other, and he did not want to have *real sex* until they got married.

Clementine said none of this to Claude. It was clear he didn't care what she thought. He told her she wouldn't get pregnant because his wife had been unable to conceive, and that according to her, he was the problem. He let Clementine know he wanted sex again when he dropped her off near her home and told her, in no uncertain terms, that if she told anyone about what they were doing, he would kill her. She believed him.

But Clementine did get pregnant. She did not want Claude to know that it was his child. When he found out she was pregnant, he called her a slut and stopped having sex with her. Clementine told her parents that the baby was not Connor's, but they didn't believe her. She kept the rape to herself.

When she told Connor she was pregnant, he was hurt and shocked. She told him she'd been raped, but he could not accept that she was pregnant by another man. He could not wrap his mind around being a father to a baby that was not his. He ended their relationship. Clementine was devastated. She cried all the time and refused to go to school. She stayed in her room and did not talk to her parents. Her hair got oily and stringy and she had to be reminded to bathe.

Clementine left the small farming village she grew up in and went to a home for unwed mothers in Biddeford Pool. Six months after giving birth to her daughter, Clementine had to move. She found a waitressing job that did not pay enough for her to support her and her daughter. She began working at sex clubs where she made more than enough money to take care of them.

Clementine kept Colette's father a secret until she met Harrison, a client at Marlow's. He was an attorney who was in the midst of leaving his wife. Every night Clementine worked he came to see her. Clementine and Harrison fell in love. It was the first time she'd been in love since Connor left her ten years before.

The last time Harrison and Clementine were together, he told her, "My wife knows I'm seeing someone, but she doesn't know who. She hired an investigator to come here and ask Jorga questions about me. I want us to meet with Jorga so we can come up with a plan."

After the three of them met, Clementine talked with Jorga about being in love with Harrison. Jorga told her how unusual it was for people in the sex-industry to actually fall in love with a client, but affirmed that it did happen. She told Clementine that she and her husband had fallen in love in just that same way and have been together for years.

Jorga told Clementine that it had been messy. *He was married and had kids. When he left his family, his wife attempted suicide, and his two girls became very protective of her. The three of them moved away and he supported the girls until they graduated from college. It was the right thing to do, and my husband always does the right thing.*

Clementine left the sex industry, although she continues to go to Marlow's five nights a week to spend the night with Harrison. Clementine is pregnant, but it's early in the pregnancy, so she's not showing. They are careful because they do not want Harrison's wife and the investigator to find out about their relationship.

Before Jorga meets with the investigator a second time, she lets her girls know that the investigator wants to meet with each of them to ask questions about Harrison. Most of the girls have been interviewed by law enforcement, so contact with the investigator is just a blip on their radar. Jorga takes care of them, and in return her girls are loyal to her. They do not tell the investigator about Clementine who leaves at 4:30 each morning or Adriana who has just left the sex trade and is writing a book.

When the investigator meets with Jorga he questions her about Harrison leaving Marlow's at 6:30 every morning. Jorga pretends to be hesitant, then says, "We have rooms here for men who want to sleep here because they don't want to go home."

Jorga shows the investigator a small room with a twin bed, a night stand, an alarm clock, and a shower. She smiles and tells him, "The men have everything they need to be able to go to work in the morning without going home."

The investigator doesn't believe that Harrison stays in one of these small rooms alone, but he can't find a viable explanation for why Harrison does spend five nights a week at Marlow's. Harrison's wife swears he's fallen in love with someone at Marlow's, but the investigator does not have any evidence to support her claim.

Months later Harrison's wife gets a call from her attorney telling her that the divorce is final. She calls Harrison's employer and they say, "No one by that name works here."

"Where's he gone?" she demands.

Human resources repeats, "No one by that name works here, ma'am."

"You're lying." She yells and slams down the phone.

The ex-wife calls the investigator, who arrives at Harrison's work place just as he's leaving the building. He follows Harrison to Alligator Alley, and on a whim, drives behind him across the swampland. Harrison goes to a new subdivision in Naples where a beautiful, pregnant woman and a young girl who looks to be about ten years old, meet him outside. The investigator remembers seeing the woman at Marlow's, although he did not interview her. Jorga told him she no longer worked at the club. The woman laughs loudly as Harrison picks her up and carries her across the threshold.

The little girl says, "Daddy, I'm glad you're finally home!"

Harrison picks her up and carries her through the doorway, too.

The investigator shakes his head and smiles as the door softly closes.

ME Diggers

Adriana

Under the red umbrella Adriana feels her heart stop. Well not really, but she does find herself gasping for air. She holds her breath and the tension in her neck and shoulders is like a taut rubber band. *Su. Oh my God! Su Williams, Billy's wife.*

Then she hears the woman say, "I'm Su. My husband and I moved to our beach house on Tybee Island two weeks ago. I'm an artist. I'm so excited about having my studio right on the ocean."

Adriana sees the resemblance to the girl Su used to be. She was always attractive in a kind of simple, country-girl way. Now she is beautiful, tan, and fit. She's dressed impeccably in hippie-like clothes, loose-fitting spring green cotton pants with a darker green tank top and a shawl of greens and blues, an ocean shawl, a work of art. She's wearing dangling blue sea-glass earrings with a matching necklace and bangles. She's taken off her shoes and stands barefoot with one leg up by her knee doing a yoga pose. She's laughing at something one of the women says. Adriana has not heard Su's laugh since high school. Adriana was MaryEllen Diggers then.

Adriana is transported back to Elizabeth's Teen Group at Liberty High School with Billy and Su. She was happy to be in the group, even though it was hard for her to show up every week and talk about herself. Being vulnerable has never been her strong suit. She had been friends with Billy since kindergarten. Having him in the group made her feel safe. Most of the time, though, she felt lonely and different. She was acutely aware of how difficult it was for her to feel connected to anyone.

Adriana is shocked to see Su here, on Long Boat Key. If Su is here, Billy is nearby. Adriana does not want to see him. She is afraid. Fear runs through her veins, just like the old days when her father would hold her down and do things to her in bed, and she had no control. She is scared for her life and doesn't want to be here anymore. She is in MaryEllen mode.

Adriana pulls down the brim on her sunhat and pushes her sunglasses up on her nose. She wants to be invisible. Before Adriana came to today's conference she was relaxed and excited about a day of art, books, yoga, and good food. Now she feels like a deer caught in the headlights.

Her girlfriend, Tami, comes back with two tall iced teas. She puts her hand on Adriana's shoulder. Adriana jumps. She doesn't want Tami's fucking hand on her shoulder. It takes everything she has to not push her hand away and get up and run. Adriana can barely breathe. Tami begins massaging Adriana's tight neck muscles. *Get your fucking hands off me,* she thinks. When Tami puts her lips on the top of Adriana's head, she abruptly gets up, nearly upsetting the table. She hears the clinking of glass and feels water dripping on her ankles. She sees a large piece of lemon on her foot and pauses, taking in how the yellow crescent looks against her orange leather sandal. Then she's moving quickly, wordlessly, away from Tami, and from Su, whose back is to her, doing the same yoga pose on the other leg now.

When Adriana gets to the sidewalk she starts running. A car swerves, barely missing her. People start honking their horns. A man yells at her in Spanish. She doesn't stop. As Adriana runs, words begin streaming through her mind.

I want to go into the cave but I'm afraid.
I want to tell you the truth but I'm scared.
I want to stop running but my feet won't stop.
I want to get a full breath of air but I can't.

In her mind she's back in Maine, running on the dirt trail in the woods behind her house. Her father is coming after her with a shot gun. Then he's on top of her, grunting and tearing at her clothes. She tells her mother, who is drunk and has a Camel cigarette hanging out of her mouth, that her father has been raping her and now she's pregnant. Her mother slaps her hard across the face and says, *You're a whore, MaryEllen. You've really done it now. Gone and got yourself pregnant. Get out of here. Leave.*

That day MaryEllen leaves Liberty with one small backpack. She is seventeen years old. She hitches a ride to Belfast, then Portland. She does not have a plan. When she gets dropped off near a hospital she goes in and talks with a social worker who finds a place for her to live at a home for unwed mothers at the monastery in Biddeford Pool. MaryEllen calls Billy and lets him know where she'll be living. She is there six months before she gives birth to her beautiful, healthy daughter, SaraLouise. MaryEllen attends school at the monastery and gets her high school diploma. She thrives. SaraLouise thrives. As MaryEllen gets closer to the time when she has to leave the monastery, she sneaks out in the middle of a cold December night and leaves SaraLouise. She calls Billy and he finds her first new name, Diana Caswell.

Adriana runs along the beach for a long time. When she finally stops, she has some clarity. She can no longer keep living this way. She has an opportunity to change her life, again. Can she stop running now? Can she look at herself? Fear rises up in her throat like ugly, black bile. Her heart rate accelerates again. She runs some more. She still has physical energy to burn. She thinks about calling Jorga, the Madam at the sex club she worked at in Miami, and returning to her old life there.

The Voice says, *Wouldn't that be doing what you always do? Oh, are we having a conversation now?*

Well, you are open now. So yes, it could be a conversation, says The Voice. *It's always an option for you to keep doing what you always do and getting the results you always get. You can only go as fast as you can go.*

Okay. I'm listening.

Your way isn't working all that well anymore, says The Voice.

That's putting it mildly. You're being nice.

You're mean enough to yourself. You don't need more of that, says The Voice.

When Adriana gets to the cottage she's been renting, she doesn't bother turning on the lights. She's a mess, sweaty blouse and skirt, blisters from her orange sandals, and she lost her hat. She feels like a groundless, formless being who is adrift, a blank slate, barren and empty. She sits in the red leather chair for a long time, not moving. Then she calls a local therapist, Lara Jorgenson. Two women from her writing group at Tami's bookstore told her Lara was good. On the third ring Lara answers.

"Hello," Lara says.

There is a long silence. Adriana thinks, *What are you doing answering your phone? I want the machine. It's Saturday night. No therapist works on a Saturday night.* She considers hanging up.

Finally, she says, "Oh, I didn't expect to get anyone."

Lara laughs. "Well, I've picked up." More silence.

"I'd like to make an appointment."

"Okay. Let me get my book. How's Monday at 10 a.m.?"

Adriana gulps and after a long pause, says, "Okay."

"So, your name." Another pause.

"Adriana." Then I stop and say, "MaryEllen Diggers."

Truths And Lies

When I get off the phone with Lara I'm shaking. I thought I was getting a Nordic woman. But no. I got another Czech! What is it with these strong Czech women? Guidance, direction, connection? They are solid. They love nature and are deeply connected to the Earth, just like Mainers. When you grow up with nature all around you, you cannot easily escape being connected to it. Nature shapes people. It shaped me. I have to calm myself down. I am too tired to run or walk. I am not too tired to write.

My parents named me MaryEllen Diggers. I'm a name-changer, a runner, a mover. I've had five names in thirty-five years, MaryEllen Diggers, Diana Caswell, Carmella Stone, Suzanne Thurman, and Adriana Tiswell. I've travelled back and forth across the United States looking for something---searching, yearning for, desiring-peace, safety, home. When you come from Maine can any other place be home? I would have said no, except I found home in the Coachella Valley, a desert community in southern California. I stayed there seven years and created a life. I hadn't stayed anywhere that long since I left Maine.

All the books say that seven years is a turning point. I had a girlfriend, Claire, for most of those seven years. I loved her. Then I ran away, again. It's like I was in a fog. I got in my car and kept driving. When I stopped at a gas station in Texas I remembered that I'd left The Box that Anna had bequeathed to me. I felt sick to my stomach and doubled over in pain. A man at the other pump asked me if I was alright. I lied and told him, *My stomach hurts. Probably too much coffee.* It was so easy for me to lie. After he drove away I called Billy. He asked me where I was going and part of me wanted to say California. I could go back to Claire. I could talk to her and have the life I wanted. Claire was a good choice. She was kind and loving and strong. She loved sex. She was a good listener. But I said, *Miami.* I sealed my fate that day. I picked up my new name when I got to Miami. Adriana Tiswell came to life. Suzanne Thurman died again.

That was the first time I had regrets about leaving. I could not bear those feelings so I got a job at Marlow's, a sex club in Miami. I was upfront with Jorga, the madam. I told her I would work there a year or two, take copious notes, and when I left I would write a book about the sex trade. Jorga and I had an understanding from the beginning. I liked Jorga. She reminded me of Anna, the Czech woman I lived with and took care of in Boston. I was Diana Caswell then.

I think about truths and lies to see if I can get to my truth.

Truth: I've had a break down or a break through. I need to sort out what's going on with me.

Truth: My heart shut down years ago.

I left my parent's house when I was seventeen years old. I was pregnant with my father's baby. I went to Portland and walked into a hospital. The staff found me a place to live in Biddeford Pool, a monastery where the nuns took in unwed mothers. I gave birth to a healthy baby girl I named SaraLouise. I loved her from the get go. She was beautiful. Her name was two names that became one, with the second name capitalized in the middle, just like mine. It's something my family does. I didn't know that it was an odd thing to do, having a capital letter in the middle of your name.

After SaraLouise's birth I could have stayed six more months at the monastery, but I got to feeling that it was too much like home, in a completely different way from my noisy, chaotic childhood home. The monastery was sterile, quiet, and there were strict rules. The nuns were nice. They provided for all my basic needs. I did chores and went to church. I wasn't Catholic, but I never felt like they were trying to convert me. I think they would have liked it if I'd converted, but I didn't have to do that to stay at the monastery. I had my own small room and shared a bathroom with another girl and her baby. There was a whole group of us girls who were pregnant and then became young mothers. We left the monastery at different times after our babies were born.

Truth: I gave my three-month-old baby away like a college text book at the end of a rough semester.

I justified leaving SaraLouise by saying if I took her with me she could die in the cold. And although there is truth in that, the bigger truth is, I could not see how I could take care of her and me.

When I left the monastery I went to Portland and had sex with men to get my basic needs met. These men were like my father. I felt like damaged goods. Then I met Jack. He was a good guy who wanted to take care of me. He went to work every day and came home at night. I was so lonely and guilt ridden and trapped that even though he was wonderful, I couldn't stay.

Truth: I had to leave Maine.

I had some crazy fear that my father would come looking for me, and when he found me, he would take me home and molest me again. And my drunk mother, with the Camel cigarette always hanging out of her mouth, would be waiting to give me the back-hand slap across the face that always came out of the blue. Then there was my younger sister, CrystalAnn, the one who bonded with them, was like them. Three against one, not a winning proposition. I don't know what happened to her. I hope she's okay.

Truth: My parents and sister were just trying to survive.

They were doing the best they could, coming from poverty, living in a harsh climate. Mom had a vegetable garden, so we had fresh food. She loved her garden. It's the only place I saw her happy. She got pregnant at seventeen, too. She married my dad and stayed. She had me, and I was like her, tough, mouthy, strong-willed. My father was an alcoholic. It's amazing I never became an addict, well, a drug addict or alcoholic. I did become a sex addict. Strange, I never got pregnant again. I've fucked so many guys. But I don't want to tell you the story of my sex addiction.

Truth: I was desperate.

I called Billy, my only friend. He gave me my first new name, Diana Caswell, and the basic details about Diana and her death. She was seven years old, from northern Wisconsin. Death by electrocution. A horrible death, no doubt. I don't know. Perhaps she died quickly. I hope so. What could the girl have been doing? Drying her baby-doll's hair? Dying in the tub with her baby-doll? Did her mother weep? Feel relieved? Was she an inattentive mother? A loving mother? Seven is old enough to take a bath by yourself.

I couldn't get Diana's death out of my mind. I wished Billy hadn't told me how she died. I never told him I didn't want to know the details about the dead girl whose name he was giving me. Every time Billy gave me a new name, he told me the girl's age, location, and how she died. He believed that by taking a dead girl's name I had an opportunity to create a new life when they didn't have a chance. He felt it was an honor.

Lie: Sex is the only place I get relief.

Nature gives me relief. Hanging laundry soothes me. Tending Anna's roses gave me relief. Anna gave me relief. She was a mother to me, a Czech mother, a loving, kind, strict mother, an encourager. I owe my life to her. I watched her die and part of me died with her. I miss her.

Truth: It's easier for me when things are black and white, yes or no, all or nothing. But in my life, nothing is that simple.

I have a hard time sleeping. I am anxious about the appointment tomorrow with Lara. Maybe I will read this to her as a way to introduce myself. It will be easier than telling her.

The Initial Meeting

"Good morning, MaryEllen. Come in."

I look around the office and see a big window and French doors that look out to the water. I see a white pelican land on a dock.

"You can sit on the couch or in the chair." Lara points to a red chair that looks a lot like mine. I sit there. I don't know what to say. Do I pull out *Truths and Lies,* the piece I wrote yesterday? I brought it with me. I glance at Lara and she sits quietly, looking at me. I turn away. She reminds me of Anna. She has a calm, strong presence. I see the quiet, stoic Eastern European in her. I feel tears behind my eyes. I don't want to cry.

Lara leans forward in the yellow leather chair. "So, MaryEllen, what brings you here today?"

What brings me here? I feel panicky. My right leg swings, so I uncross my legs and place both feet on the floor. I want to take off my shoes and curl my feet under me, but I don't. I'm usually full of words, but not today. I'm having a hard time even looking at her. I feel like getting up and leaving, bolting out those French doors and running on the beach.

"I don't know what to say."

"What happened on Saturday?" Lara asks.

What happened on Saturday? My whole life tilted, toppled, shifted. What the fuck? I feel incredibly anxious. I want to get up and run. I say, "I couldn't do what I always do."

"And what do you always do?" Lara asks.

"I run."

"Run?"

"Well, on Saturday, I physically ran away from the conference after I saw Su, Billy's wife."

"So you saw Su and had to leave." Lara says it calmly. "And who are Su and Billy to you?"

Who are Su and Billy to me? Oh my God! I stare at her. She stares back. "People from my past." I say it matter-of-factly and with attitude. I hope that I have left no room for conversation. I am trying to hold onto something here. I thought I'd surrendered, but here I am, word-sparring.

"People from your past." She repeats what I say in the same tone that I used. And then we sit there. I get the feeling she's not going to rescue me. Even though I pushed her away, I do not know if I really want her away.

Lara surprises me when she says, "Do you want to tell me more about them?"

Yes and no. Fear washes over me. "I do and I don't." *This is fucking ridiculous. What am I waiting for here?* I look at Lara. She is leaning forward slightly.

"I've never been to a therapist before."

"What makes you want to be here now?" She says.

"I don't know if I want to be here now, but I feel like I need to be here. I don't even know if that's true. I don't like to need anybody or anything."

"So you feel like you may need to be here?"

"Maybe. Needing hasn't gotten me anything but bad."

"You've been good at keeping your needs at bay," Lara says.

I look at her to see if she's fucking with me. She doesn't seem to be. "Yes. I guess you could say that's true."

"So, what need brought you here, MaryEllen?"

I stare at her. She keeps her eyes on mine. *We've been doing a word dance, a fucking weird, stilted conversation because I won't just come out and say what's going on.*

"Look. I'm not liking this conversation or whatever we're doing here. I feel like I'm holding on. Like I'm afraid to open up, because if I do, the flood gates will open and maybe I'll be tumbled around, hurt, or killed."

"Life and death are at risk here." Lara says.

"Yes. If I talk about my life I could die, but if I don't talk about my life I could die."

"That's quite a bind."

"Yeah. Tell me about it."

Lara asks, "Why don't you tell me about Su and Billy?"

I look at her and feel her caring. I dive in.

"Su and Billy and I grew up in Liberty, Maine. It's a little town about fifteen miles from the coast. The three of us were in a teen group together in high school. Billy and I were friends. We used to play in the woods and go hunting. When Su and Billy got together I liked Su, but we were never friends.

"So what happened when you saw Su?"

"If Su was there, Billy was somewhere near, and I didn't want to see him."

"You didn't want to see your friend?"

"It's like I thought something bad might happen. I got scared."

"What do you know about your fear?"

"Like I'd be back being MaryEllen. I left her behind years ago." My throat tightens and I start to cry. In my head I think: *If I look at this amorphous crap, this life of mine in Liberty, I might go crazy. I might end up in a mental hospital.* I shake my head, "This is all a little crazy."

"So you're afraid of going crazy, being crazy?"

You don't know the half of it. I am silent.

Lara sits quietly looking at me. I can barely sit still. It's like she's waiting for me to break the silence. We sit longer.

Lara asks in a soft voice, "You left MaryEllen behind years ago?"

"Yeah. When I left Maine, Billy gave me my first new name, Diana Caswell. I was eighteen years old. I've had five names in thirty-five years. Who does that?" I begin to cry really hard.

Lara sits with me in this quiet space while I cry. *Compassion does not ooze out of her, but I do feel cared about. I don't want someone soothing me. I didn't get that as a child and I don't trust it. When I see children crying in the grocery store and their mothers are comforting them, I don't understand it. These mothers hold them and assure them that all is well even though they are not getting what they want. What is that? Something I don't understand. Isn't it normal to feel angry or disappointed when you don't get what you want? I don't want someone to soothe me. What's the point? I'm still not going to get what I want. Let me have my feelings and I'll move on.* Two birds at the bird feeder start squawking. Both want to be fed. And only one of them can eat at a time. I laugh.

Lara laughs too, and says, "Everybody wants to get their needs met."

I nod and ask, "Can I read you *Truths and Lies* ?"

She nods and says, "There may not be time to talk about it this session, but I can listen."

"That'll work for me."

She smiles. She doesn't have to say the obvious, *I'm sure it will.*

The Encounter

After my appointment with Lara, I go home. I sit in my red chair with a notepad and pen. I look out at the waves and see a dolphin swim by. I hear words. I start writing. If I go back to Lara, I will read her these words at my next appointment.

Running through the woods
The girl runs with her backpack banging against her back
Running
She feels the presence behind her
Will it catch her this time?
Will she let it?
Last week she ran like the wind
And he could not get her
She had not wanted to be gotten
Cat and mouse
She had escaped with her life
She knows this is true
This time though
She wants something different
She wants to meet the presence
The man in all his darkness
He wants to connect with her
He has something to say
She is ready to listen
She wants to hear
She slows down her running
When she comes to the river
She strips off her clothes
She enters the cool waters
The dark presence greets her
They swim together
Encloaked in the dark green of morning light
She feels a freedom she has never felt
A comfort she has not known
She and the dark presence become one
She is glad to have stopped running

She is glad to be home in fertile waters
Singing

I guess I'm going back to therapy. I am ready to be MaryEllen Diggers again, for a while at least.

My Brick Wall

We all have our brick wall. We all come up against something at some time in our lives that catches us short, that causes us to stop. We are taken by surprise at the strength of our feelings and thoughts. Our old coping mechanisms no longer work. We try managing and that doesn't work either. We are crawling out of our skins and can't seem to get comfortable or we can't stop moving. A different sort of person will become inert, nearly catatonic, two sides of the same coin.

After the earthquake comes:

Person #1: begins frenzied activity and cleaning up. Desperately wants to make order out of chaos.

Person #2: sits in the chair with destruction all around. Cannot take any action. Is stuck in the chair. Can barely keep her eyes open. Ruin is everywhere.

Take your pick. They are merely two different ways of handling a stressful situation.

So what is your brick wall? What does it represent? What is your relationship with this wall? Is it a fortress? Is it a small barrier that anyone can get over? Is there a rose garden in the middle of the courtyard? Are you trying to keep people out? Are you safe within the walls? You will let people in or you won't. It's your choice.

This brick wall stands in the middle of the desert
A fortress
There is no sentry at the gate
There is no gate
There is a blue wooden door inviting me in
If I dare
If I must
I come to portals
I walk through or I don't
And even if I walk through
I may stand by the door and find myself unable to move
I watch the door close
I stand on the other side
Speechless

Wordless
Fear ripples through my body
I know nothing
I have entered a new space
Eyes wide open
Alert
Startled when the eagle flies by
I watch her land in a tree
She turns
I watch her watching me
Our staring leaves me breathless
My heart begins to pound
I have no bearings
I push to see if the door will open
But I already know it won't

I heard the 3 clicks after I walked through
I chose
Now I must deal with myself
The brick wall appears in front of me

Claire

Invitation To Stay

It has been 730 days since my partner, Suzanne, went missing. She has not returned and there has been no contact. None. No sightings. Poof! Here one day and gone the next. I still find myself waiting for her. I don't know how long I can keep living with not knowing Suzanne's whereabouts. I am heartbroken and I desperately need solace. Suzanne was there one morning, then she did not come home that night or any night after that. I eventually contacted the police and reported Suzanne missing. I did not want to make that report because I did not know if Suzanne was really missing.

Today I hike on a trail I have never taken before. After several hours I see a brick wall. Some of the bricks are crumbling, but the wall is in surprisingly good shape, intact, clearly still a wall. After I walk along its exterior for at least an hour, I come to a blue door hanging from one hinge. I go through this entryway and follow a stone path that ends at a well-maintained cottage. On the outside of the cottage is a plaque that says: *Vitejte Svobody Chate*. The cottage door is red, and there's a note in a clear plastic cover tacked onto it. I take it out and read it.

Welcome to Freedom Cottage
Invitation to Stay

Dobre Rano,

I encourage each visitor to make good use of the rich library of books and art that are here. The table made of hewn oak is perfect for writing, reading, having a cup of tea or coffee. You can use the yellow kettle on the gas stove, and there is a wide assortment of teas and coffees in colored tins on the counter. The orange glass water pitcher with white polka-dots and two matching water glasses makes it easy to keep hydrated. Make yourself at home. Stay overnight if you desire. Peace, Milos

I walk through the red door. I fall in love with the cottage from the moment I enter it. Light streams in the windows. Books in built-in-bookcases sit ready for the taking. I love the colorful polka-dotted dishes that are stamped with *Made in East Germany*. I hear birds chirping and splashing in the birdbath and see the fire pit in the yard surrounded by large rocks. I hear the wind chimes ring as the wind begins to blow. I spend the night and have the best sleep I've had since Suzanne disappeared. I dream of a boy playing in flower-filled fields with the sun shining. He's happy, laughing, and content. I wake up smiling for the first time in two years. I didn't realize how much I've missed these long, deep, dream-filled sleeps.

I begin to stay at the cottage every weekend. I feel at home here. As I explore the outside area I find *Milo's Story* etched into the bricks on the inside of the wall. I walk the entire wall and then I begin to read his story.

After spending a month at Freedom Cottage, I contact a realtor and ask about buying the property. The odd thing is, the realtor cannot find evidence that the property exists.

I return to the cottage. I know someone is maintaining the house because the *Welcome to Freedom Cottage* note that was tacked on the door in clear plastic, is gone. There are fresh daffodils in a blue glass vase on the oak table with a note in an envelope that simply says *CLAIRE*.

In the note, Milos offers me the property. He asks me to read his entire etched story on the bricks, write it down, and publish it. I want to do this. Before I leave the cottage I write a big *YES* on the note, *yes* to writing the story and *yes* to moving here.

I give notice on my apartment and begin packing. I find a box as I am packing. In it is MaryEllen Diggers' Birth Certificate, four glass marbles, a large red chunk of sea glass, a baby picture with SaraLouise written on the back, and Anna McClean's obituary.

After living many years as a paraplegic due to a skiing accident, Anna McClean died last night. She leaves one daughter, Janna Rodriguez, her four-year-old twin grandchildren, and her brother, Milos Czechkowski. Anna was the founder of Decklin Place, a facility dedicated to helping people recover from spinal cord injuries. For the past twenty years Anna helped people work through grief and loss issues so they could transition into a new life. Her death is a huge loss to the recovery community. Anna will be missed by her family, friends, and community.

I have no idea what to make of the box. I remember the day Suzanne found a large chunk of red sea glass, and excitedly talked about how unusual it was to find any red sea glass, particularly a piece that was so large. Could this be the same piece? It looks like it, but I didn't look at it that closely when Suzanne showed it to me.

Could the box have belonged to Suzanne? I am curious about the box and its contents. I contact my landlady to see if the box is hers. When she says no, I pack the box.

Several months later I find the box when I'm unpacking and put it on the bookshelf. It is a beautiful, dark brown wooden box with a large silver leaf on top. And even though I do not understand the box's contents, I have a strong intuition that the box belongs to Suzanne.

One year after I move into Freedom Cottage, I get an early-morning knock on the red door. It is an unexpected visitor, an elderly man with curly grey hair peeking out from his black wool cap and a twinkle in his eye. He bows slightly and greets me with *dobre rano, good morning* in Czech. Milos has come for a visit.

The Meeting

After Milos says *Dobre rano,* I gasp and grab his hand. I can't believe he's here. "Milos! Good Morning. I'm so glad you're here. I wondered when I'd meet you. Come in, come in. Make yourself comfortable. Can I get you a cup of tea or coffee?"

"Yes, coffee please, black."

As I go to make the coffee I watch Milos look around. I've been here a year now and I've certainly made Freedom Cottage my own. The large table by the window that serves as my desk has spectacular views of the mountains and the vast open space. Milos' story is spread out all over the table.

He says, "I see you are working hard."

"Yes," I say as I bring him his coffee in the orange and white polka-dotted cup. "I hope you like it strong."

"Is there any other way to take coffee?" he says with a twinkle in his eyes.

"Not for me," I say. "When I was in college in Vermont I came upon a Turkish coffee house and that was where I began drinking coffee. Before that, I'd tasted my parent's coffee, but it was weak. I didn't think I liked coffee." I laugh. "I learned that was a lie. I began to go every day to that coffee house. The coffee was alluring."

Milos says, "I'm not sure of the purpose of weak coffee, but it's not my cup of tea either."

We sit. There is a quiet comfort and a silence that I appreciate and have gotten used to since I've been living here.

Milos tells me, "My grandfather came from Czechoslovakia and my family settled in Boston. My grandfather was a traveler and he came west on one of his many trips. He found the desert alluring. It was a time when homesteading was an option. You had to live on the land for four years and then it was yours. Grandpa was very invested in this land and the Indian culture. My father was born in this house. But his mother wanted to raise her son in Boston. Education was important to her. After four years, they moved back to Boston and came out here for extended vacations. I remember making the bricks with my grandfather and my father for the brick wall. More people were heading west and coming to this valley. My grandfather wanted to make the boundaries of his land clear.

As a teenager, I spent one summer here writing my story on these brick walls. My parents and my sister, Anna, had gone back to Czechoslovakia for the summer. I wanted to be in the desert with my grandpa. I was alone with him. We didn't know that my grandpa was dying at the time."

Milos stops talking and looks around the room. I see his eyes get wide. He says in a pressured tone, "Where did you get that box?"

I get up and bring the box to the table. I say, "I found it in the back of my closet when I was packing up to move here. I'd never seen it before. I asked my landlady if it was hers and she said no. I packed it up."

Milos says, "It looks like a box my sister had. A Czechoslovakian artist made hers. Anna gave it to her daughter, Janna, but Janna did not want it, which was a great source of disappointment and upset to my sister. Anna gave it to Diana, a young woman who took care of her the last six years of her life."

I look at him surprised. "Anna McClean? Her obituary was in the box."

Milos looks at me quizzically. He opens the box and looks inside the lid and says, "This is Anna's box. See the letters AMC. She wrote them in. They stand for Anna Marie Czechkowski. My mother was so angry that she did that. What else was in the box?"

I say, "A birth certificate for MaryEllen Diggers, a baby picture with SaraLouise on the back of it, four marbles, and a big red chunk of sea glass. I think the box may have belonged to my girlfriend, Suzanne. I don't really know."

Milos looks at me and says, "Anna gave this box to Diana Caswell."

I stare at him and ask, "Do you know MaryEllen Diggers or SaraLouise?"

"I don't. I haven't seen or heard from Diana since she left Boston. She took my Death and Dying class at Harvard at Anna's request and then she disappeared.

I put down my coffee and repeat, "she disappeared?"

"Yes," Milos says. "Diana was devastated by Anna's death. They were very close. I hoped Diana might stay and get her PhD.

She was smart. She got her Bachelors and Masters while she worked for Anna."

I look at Milos. I feel shell-shocked and confused. I get up, get the photo album, and open it.

He says, "That's Diana."

I say, "That's Suzanne. She disappeared two years ago."

Milos says quietly, "We seem to have ourselves a mystery."

I stare at him as tears roll down my cheeks.

The Bird On The Wire

Milos and I sit in stunned silence. I hear the noisy ravens and imagine they are in the palo verde tree. I see the yellow bird sitting quietly on the wire that holds my wind chimes. She showed up about a week ago. I can't remember exactly when she came. I could look it up in my green leather journal if I was so inclined. I have the documentation. But that's just it, I don't feel inclined. I feel like her days are numbered here, but I don't know if that's true. What is true, is, she was here yesterday and she is here today. The little yellow bird has endeared herself to me.

I hope she will be here tomorrow. But that's the hitch in the whole thing. I don't know about tomorrow. I only know about today and yesterday. Not knowing is bothering me.

Most every morning I get up and put words on blank white pages. It is my daily ritual. I am a writer. It is what writers do. Not yesterday though. I put no words on paper yesterday. I thought about a trip I took with Suzanne the week before she disappeared. I took my journal along, but I never got to my writing. It sat in my bag, clearly not my priority.

I wish I could talk to Suzanne about Fluffy, which is short for fluffy-little-yellow-bird-on-the-wire. On that trip I was enamored with a bird that looked a lot like Fluffy. I spent a lot of time watching her. Suzanne was interested in her too, but I was the one who needed to talk at length about the bird. Suzanne listened to me and it seemed like she was taking me seriously, which was unusual for her because she liked to keep things light and breezy. Mostly I liked that about her because I am way too serious for my own good.

I remember Suzanne laughing and saying, *She's a bird on a wire, Claire. That's it.* I was quiet for a minute reflecting upon what she said. *I don't agree.* That's when the conversation changed. Suzanne groaned. I didn't disagree with her very often because when I did we had a fight or there was distance. It was a lose-lose proposition. But sometimes you just have to stand by what you say. Some things matter. That's how it is.

When Suzanne and I were together, we woke up nearly every morning and mixed it up in and out of bed. We drank strong coffee together. When I began to meditate and write every morning, which cut into our time in bed, she didn't like it. I wonder if that's why she disappeared. The last thing she said to me was, *I'm sick of playing second fiddle to your meetings, meditation, writing, and yoga, Claire.* I was stunned. I turned and walked away from her without saying a word. I practiced restraint. I went to work and my Wednesday 5:30 p.m. women's meeting. I never saw her again.

Six months after Suzanne disappeared I no longer believed that she had been hurt or taken. I began to say to people, *she left me.* I burnt her papers and cut up her clothes. I could not take them to the Goodwill because I did not want to see anyone else wearing them. I did not have good will. I had rage.

Today is the two-year anniversary of Suzanne's leaving. I have a life again. I love living at Freedom Cottage. I have been working on Milo's book and am close to finishing it. This project and my 12-step program have saved my life.

I look up when I hear the chimes start to ring. I see Fluffy sitting right on the wire looking at me. *I'm attached to you, you little sucker. Don't leave me now.*

I turn to Milos who is also looking at Fluffy.

He says quietly, "I love the yellow ones. When I was a boy, I loved when the yellow ones came. We only got one at a time. I never understood this and I wanted to understand. I thought she might be lonely and I worried about her. But that's a story I made up. I've come to believe that some of us are meant to have a solo journey. I do not understand that either, but I am more accepting of that possibility now. I believe it is one of the reasons I delved into grief and death and dying. I needed to understand loss. Studying and teaching the subject have enabled me to have conversations that most people do not want to have. American culture does not know how to deal with loss effectively. I believe coming from Czechoslovakia, and perhaps any Eastern European country, gave me a perspective that Americans do not acquire easily. When there is no escape from seeing loss on nearly a daily basis, one is reminded how the cycle of life works. Its impact is profound. There is grief, yes, and there is acceptance that loss and death are merely a part of life. Loss is. Death is. Here in America it is as though loss is in a category that does not want to be claimed, territory that does not want to be visited, and in fact most people deny its existence. Be happy. Pretend something does not exist. That is the American creed." He pauses and looks at Fluffy and then me.

"I've named her Fluffy, short for fluffy-little-yellow-bird-on-the-wire. I love her. I don't want her to leave." I begin to cry.

"Aah, my dear Claire. Perhaps a trip to Maine to find out more about MaryEllen Diggers is in order."

I nod and take his hand.

Claire's Dream: Fighting For Her Life

After Milos leaves, I am restless and exhausted. I fall asleep on the couch and have this dream.

I pick up the knife. Do I need protection? Is this a last-ditch attempt to slay the dragons, to fight the fight, to not roll over, to not be beat down? Except I am beat down. It's been a long fight. Is this what my self-soothing is about? I wonder if I'm using physical comfort to manage myself. Or is this just my crazy thinking taking over again?

The voices inside my head battle. *Don't try to calm me down and shut me up. Don't touch me! Your touch feels patronizing. Be voiceless. I'll soothe you. No! I will not be quiet. I can't let you win.* I am tired of feeling defenseless.

I join a debate team where I shout and defend myself with angry words. Word-fighting. The good old days, but not really, because I am always left wanting and unsatisfied. I can't get behind the words. I join a gym and begin boxing.

I am now a boxer fighting in the middle of the ring. When the bell rings I return to my corner to lick my wounds and be tended to. When the bell rings again they push me back into the ring for the next round. I get beat up badly that first fight. The other woman does too.

I win that fight, except it doesn't feel like a victory. I knock the woman down more times than she knocks me down. I get more punches in, connect with the woman's face more times than the woman connects with my face. When I look in the mirror I don't recognize my bruised, bloody, swollen face.

For a while I have the fight in me. No more. I am done, but I don't feel better. I'm still not satisfied. I feel empty and tired and weary, just like I did when I slaughtered people with socially acceptable, middle class, white-bread words. People didn't get physically hurt, but they got emotionally, mentally, and spiritually damaged. I find out that replacing words with physical aggression does not take my pain away. I have not made a shift. I have no resolution. I am not dealing with my underlying issues.

I examine the knife in my hand. I finger the sharp blade. I love the glistening stainless steel. I see my ravaged face in the blade, my wild eyes those of a feral animal. I want to run and hide.

What do I really want to do with the knife? Am I going to cut someone, slash someone, kill someone? Or maybe I'll turn the knife on myself, make an attempt to cut myself open. But what good would that do? Besides needing stitches and a trip to the Emergency Room, what purpose would it serve? Even if I try to cut out this old, ugly rotting part of myself, it won't work, because it's in my mind. No physical injury can take my pain away.

I have read that surrender is part of the spiritual solution to every problem. I think that might be true, but I have difficulty believing that some force I cannot see, will actually help me. I do believe in energy, though, because I feel its vibrations and shifts. Lately my energy has been dark and edgy and angry. I feel put upon. I have the desire to be alone because relationships are too much work, and I cannot stand being touched.

I drop the knife and kick it across the room. I fall to my knees and pray.

I wake up with a start to squawking ravens. I do not see Fluffy.

Eliza

The Buddha File

On a Tuesday night in the library I unexpectedly come upon The Buddha File buried in the art section between the thick books of Cezanne and Chagall. It does not have a number and it is not in the card catalogue. I wonder what it's doing here. I take the file to one of the small wooden tables and begin to read.

> *My Dearest,*
> *Since you have found The Buddha File, I invite you to read the file in its entirety and leave me your feedback on the enclosed forms. I have been working on this project for the past three years and have collected dozens of responses. Soon I will have all the feedback I need to complete my dissertation. You are integral to my success. Your anonymous responses matter to me. You will make a difference to my project.*
> *Let me tell you how this began. I wanted to explore the nature of impermanence. I did not understand how some people embrace this concept almost immediately and others, like myself, struggled with it.*
> *You may be asking, what are the truths about impermanence? Words like changing, flowing, and nothing ever stays the same, come to mind. Always there is movement, shifting energy.*
> *For some of us there is a desire to keep things the same. That is my problem. I was very unhappy because I could not successfully keep things the same. And God knows, I tried.*
> *When I came upon the story that I've included in this file, something happened deep inside me.*
> *Much gratitude and appreciation,*
>
> *The Man*

I turn the page and begin reading the story.

> *She came upon the crack before she knew it. It isn't like she hadn't been told because she had. But-she hadn't believed. She couldn't believe because if she did her whole world would be*

shattered. That was her thought. Shattered. Like glass raining onto her, pouring over her, and she getting cut by the jagged edges and caressed by the round smooth polished pieces. So, you see, it isn't simple. This raining glass hurts and doesn't hurt, cuts and doesn't cut. And she finds herself standing as though she's under a glass waterfall, and the power of the water overwhelms her. She bleats out a cry. She moans when the cut is deep. She laughs when a green round polished stone caresses her eyes. So many feelings at once. She isn't managing well. She sees only what she wants to see. Pretending. Making up a story to tell. A nice story. A story people want to hear. She's playing the game. Because who wants to hear the story of the sharp, raining glass that cracked her wide open?

I am stunned. Then I notice wet spots on the paper. I become aware that I am crying. On the feedback form I write that I am tired of pretending, that I have been feeling lost for a long time, and that I want to find another way to be. I write my name and phone number and put the file back where I found it. I feel hope. I want The Man to contact me.

Four Corners

I sit in the white room and look at the piles of crap in each of the four corners. I don't know how the piles got here, but I do know they've grown taller over time and lean like The Leaning Tower of Pisa. If I add anything else to the towers they might tumble and I don't want them to fall. I think about Blockhead, the game I played as a child, placing colored wooden blocks of various shapes on top of each other. The point of the game was to take turns placing the blocks on top of each other and not have the blocks fall.

These piles here have books, paper, trinkets, clothes, and God knows what else. In the Northeast corner, there is a metal sculpture of a girl sitting on a swing. I don't remember putting that sculpture on top of the pile. In the Northwest corner, there's a jack-in-the-box. The Southeast corner has a mobile of bells that ring and move like a fan blows them, but I've never seen a fan here. In the Southwest corner, there's a music box playing *The Rites of Spring* with a dancing ballerina that begins to move when music is piped in. The lithe girl in the pink tutu spins. There seems to be no rhyme or reason to when or why this happens. I know I am not supposed to touch the towers in the corners. I only know the directions because the corners are labeled. There is something about the towers that I like, but I have been feeling increasingly discontent.

I don't know why I'm in this room again and what these piles are doing here. I don't remember coming here. I think I was drugged. As my energy returns, I begin to think more clearly. I am trying to find patterns. I haven't been able to see any. I know I've been here at least twenty-one days because twenty-one days ago I began making small tick marks on the floor that The Man doesn't seem to notice. Three times a day, through a hole in the door, The Man gives me a tray of good healthy food, mostly juices and salads. I like the food.

Today paper and paint appear, and I paint. I remember I like to paint and I'm good at it. I paint a large picture of a green cottage on a lake. The details of the cottage spark my memory. I vaguely recollect The Man coming to that cottage unexpectedly, knocking on the door in the early evening, saying he was lost, and I let him in. I paint a picture of The Man and hold it up when I finish it, like show and tell. After I show my picture, the lights go out and the room is completely black. It stays black for a long time. In the darkness I do yoga postures-warrior one, downward dog, and standing tree pose. I do my Vipassana meditation cross-legged on the bed.

After I stop meditating, I lie down, and my mind is quiet. Quieting my mind is what I've learned to do these past twenty-one days. After what seems like a long time, the lights in the corners flash on. A large drummer boy bangs his small drum, and a video talks about acceptance, surrender, and suffering.

As strange as it seems, I am not suffering. I am lonely, the same as when I was living in the cottage. In this white room I cannot escape my loneliness. There is piped-in music, bell sounds, and lights that blink on and off. I have no control over what happens to me. I have begun to talk out loud and ask questions. I get no response.

In the quiet I remember the Four Corners sign when my family passed through there years ago. My father was driving, and all of us kids were piled in the back of the cream-colored '57 Chevy station wagon. Soon after we passed the sign, the car went off the road and into the lake. I don't know how I got to shore. No one else in my family survived. I finally fell asleep and when I woke up in the morning I was cold, stiff, and alone. There was no trace of the car or my family. I sat all day and finally accepted that no one was coming. Then I stayed another night because I didn't know what else to do. As I watched the sun go down, the mosquitoes came again. I slept fitfully and dreamed about the crash. I heard my brothers and sisters screaming and remembered the silence as the car filled with water.

That second morning, as daylight came, I woke with my heart pounding. I saw a road I hadn't noticed the day before. Soon after I got to the road, a young couple picked me up and took me to the police station. Detective Jim Brandt listened to my story. He gave me food and clothes, and I took a shower. He sent officers out to where I said the car went off the road. I stayed at the police station all day.

I was fourteen years old and smart. I saw that Detective Brandt was having difficulty believing my story. He said there was no evidence of a car having gone off the road. I kept telling him the same story over and over. Detective Brandt took me to his home that night. After dinner, his wife, May, took me to the guest room. I was safe and had a room of my own that night.

The next morning Detective Brandt contacted the FBI. They came and interviewed me. I told them I didn't remember where I came from. They never found the '57 Chevy in the lake.

I lived with May and Jim for four years. They sent me for therapy but I never told my story. I never talked about the accident. After I graduated with honors from Four Corner's High School, I attended Vassar College, about three hours from home. In an English class, I wrote a story that unintentionally revealed something about my former life. My professor, Madeline Allen, believed I was telling the truth when I wrote that I had escaped from The Man. I took Madeline into my confidence. She was the first person I trusted since I escaped from The Man.

Madeline asked me if she could send my story to the school paper. I agreed to let my story be published under a pseudonym.

It has been four years since my short story was first published in the college paper. I'm twenty-five now. I'm a writer for a small-town newspaper. Recently my short story has been republished and this time it gets nationwide coverage. I feel scared and vulnerable. I call Madeline and she agrees to keep my shocking memoir, *Four Corners,* in her safe. If I disappear, Madeline will contact the newspaper and the police, and she will publish my memoir.

Soon after my conversation with Madeline, The Man shows up at my door. My guard is down and I don't check to see who is at the door before I open it.

Once again, I am here in the white room. My mission is to find my way out again. And I will, because that's the game, isn't it? The jack-in-the-box pops up and down, the bells ring, the swing in the metal sculpture creaks, and the light flashes on and off my picture of The Man. There is no escaping these bells and whistles in the four corners.

I lie on the bed no longer hearing the sounds from the four corners. I might die, but I will win in the end. My story will be told. The Man will be found. I wait for my next meal and the rescuers who I believe will soon find me.

Eliza's Escape

One minute you and I are standing together on the bridge watching the fast- moving river, and then I watch you fall into the water. I hear you scream as the water quickly envelopes you. I stare at the back of your bobbing head as the fast-moving water carries you downstream. You're gone. My legs are shaking, and I feel cold water on my feet. I see the remaining slats of the old wooden bridge.

I snap into survival mode. I better cross the bridge and get to land before I'm washed away too. I claw my way up the bank. I hold onto loose mud and newly exposed roots. I hear the old bridge creaking. I turn when I reach the knoll. The bridge is gone. I can barely see its timbers as the water quickly pushes them down stream.

I'm scared. I see your car on the other side, something I didn't consider when I was on the bridge, but it doesn't matter now. I'm out here with the rain pouring down and the river rapidly rising. I'm soaking wet. I feel my beating heart and wet body. I make it to the top of the bank. I am safe here, for now.

The heat of the night is still strong. Even with no sun it's probably in the triple digits. I wonder where I'll go. I have no idea where I am. You brought me here and now you're gone. I can't grasp any of this. My tears blend with the rain water, and I taste the salt in my mouth.

I start running and my pink tennis shoes go squish, squish, squish. I keep losing the road and eventually I'm running in soggy sand. When I stop running, I realize I am free from The Man.

The Postage Stamp

As I run up the stairs to my fifth-floor walk-up, I pass a mailman on the second floor landing who's coming down with one of those carts you put packages on when they're too heavy to carry. It isn't Tom, the regular mail guy, who I would have stopped to talk to because that's what we do if we happen to meet on the stairs. We've been doing it for ten years.

I continue running, and when I turn the corner, I see a large box sitting in front of my door. My heart is pounding. Perhaps there's a mistake. No one except Tom knows I live here, and he isn't really a friend because I don't have friends. I have acquaintances and work colleagues and people I fuck, but never here, and they certainly don't know where I live. I don't receive mail here. I have P.O. Box 259, NY, NY 10003. Anonymous. Completely anonymous.

I walk gingerly up to the large box wrapped in plain white paper, with red, blue, and yellow tape patterned like a Mondrian painting, perfect for Art Historian, Marissa Sloan, but I'm wary. I don't see any name or address until I turn it over. I gasp. Printed in neat tiny black calligraphy is Eliza Sloan. I have not been Eliza for the past ten years. When I escaped, I left that woman and her life behind.

The large stamp looks like a Degas painting, ballerinas dancing in pink tutus. When I examine the stamp more closely, I see it's a reproduction of the music box from the Southwest corner of the white room where The Man held me in captivity. Questions flood my mind and fear races through my veins. Did The Man take the music box and make it into a French stamp? How is that possible? I thought The Man died.

I unlock the six locks on the door, push the package in and shut the door behind me. I click the locks back into place and check the windows, closets, and underneath the bed. Clear.

I stand quietly looking out the window and see the mailman I passed on the stairs with his back to me. He's taken his hat off and my stomach clenches. I turn to open the package when I hear a click and Stravinsky's *The Rites of Spring* fills the room. I stop in my tracks. Today is the ten-year anniversary of my escape from The Man, and he has found me. When I open the package, I see a

---

81

beautiful bronze and wood replica of the green cottage on the lake from my painting, with the addition of The Man sitting next to me on the porch.

I open the note.

Yes! I got your drawing made into a postage stamp. You and me forever, Eliza.

I run to the window. The Man is staring up at me with that crazy grin on his face! I turn and hit speed dial to Detective Brandt, and then Madeline. I am *not* giving up my life again.

New York

Jagged Edges

I kill the deer in the wild and skin her. I cut her flesh into large chunks with the serrated knife. I have trouble making the chunks of meat the same size. I don't know why this bothers me today. It's never bothered me before. Her blood is bothering me too.

I don't like seeing the dead deer. Right here in the middle of the woods with bright white snow surrounding me, I cut out her heart and eat it raw. It tastes rubbery, and I have to chew each piece a long time before I can swallow it. As I eat, the deer's blood drips onto the snow. I wipe my face with my hand and see red streaks on my hands and forearms. I pick up clean new snow to wash my face and hands. I feel connected to the dead deer after eating her heart.

I'm running out of time. I must get out of here before dusk when the foxes, coyotes, and cats come out to play and hunt. I do not want them hunting me. I put the chunks of deer meat into baggies and stuff them in my backpack. I get out of the woods before dark.

The next day when I'm at work my co-worker comes to my cubicle and says, "I heard your edgy tone. Were you talking to a customer?"

"What are you doing listening to my conversations?" I say loudly.

"Whoa, Ben. What's going on with you?"

"I don't like you in my business. You're not my boss."

She looks at me and says, "Did something happen this weekend?"

I say in a low, barely controlled voice, "That's none of your fucking business. Stop listening to my conversations."

"You told me you were going hunting this weekend."

I stare blankly at her. I stab my pencil into the pad of paper sitting on my desk. "Go away. Now!"

As she turns to leave, she says, "You have a lot of jagged edges, Benjamin Stoller."

I want to cut her with the serrated knife and watch her take her last breath. I want to cut out her tongue, slash her breasts, and get to her beating heart and stuff it in my mouth. I want to eviscerate her just like I did the deer this past weekend.

I sit at my desk as I hear my co-workers leave for lunch. When I hear the familiar silence of the office, which I normally like, I breathe a sigh of relief. It isn't like usual though. I know I'm in trouble. I write my boss a note letting her know that I have a family emergency. I tell her I don't know when I'll be back. I move quickly down twenty flights of stairs so I will most likely not run into anyone. Luckily, I don't. I breathe a sigh of relief. I head to the subway. I don't take a cab because I don't want to be in a position to have to talk with anyone. If I could walk all the way home I would, but it's too far. I want to blend into the mass of humanity where no one really looks at, or sees, anybody. It's why I moved to New York City.

As I get to my fifth-floor walk-up I see the mailman leaving a large box outside my neighbor's door. I want to slash his throat, watch him bleed, and eat his still beating heart. I quietly let myself in and breathe another sigh of relief. I am glad to be alone.

I thought my rage was over after I killed my mother and then my father.

I know how to cut and kill. You taught me that, Dad. When I was seven years old you left me in that cold cabin to teach me a lesson. I learned it. Hate and self-preservation. When you returned, I submitted to you-your will and your big penis going in and out of my anus and you driving it in me and calling out Mom's name. I tore that first time, bright red blood that you made me clean up by licking it. Then I had to suck your big penis until you came in my mouth. How many years of this, Dad? Seven. And Mom knew, and she couldn't protect me. You raped her too, but I realized you liked it better with me. You could do anything you wanted with me. I was small and helpless.

I saw you tie Mom up one night when you thought I was sleeping. You butt-fucked her and stuck a rag in her mouth, so when she screamed I wouldn't wake up. You'd already been going at me for four years by then. I was only ten years old. I tried to talk to Mom about it, but she wouldn't listen.

I can't leave. She said.

Why? I asked.

It's complicated, Benjamin.

He's hurting me, Mom.

I'm sorry, Ben. I'm afraid if I try to leave him he'll find us and kill us. I don't want you to die, Ben.

Please, Mom.

And her answer was, *I'm too sick, Ben. I can't leave.*

I never understood the whole set up, Mom. I did not want to kill you. You were bed-ridden by then, and nearly every day you asked me to take you out of your misery. I said *no* many times, and then, I said *yes*. You squeezed my hand as the pills worked their magic. I sat with you in the quiet of that afternoon. I sat with you until you stopped breathing. When I heard the clock strike 4:00 I knew I had to get on with the business at hand.

Dad got home early that day. I don't know why. He walked in on me bagging your flesh, Mom. I saw his look of horror and knew he would call the police, and I wasn't having it. I attacked him with the serrated knife.

I enjoyed killing Dad. I tied him up just like he did you and me, Mom. I anally raped him. He shouted expletives. I enjoyed his pain and suffering. I lost respect for him years ago. He got what he deserved. I cut his penis off and stuffed it in his mouth.

As I watched him bleed out, I took his shriveled penis out of his mouth and he whispered, *God will punish you.*

No! I said as I stuffed his penis back in his mouth. *No, Dad. It's an eye for an eye. Isn't that how it works?*

I cut him up, Mom. I burned his flesh in the wood stove. I didn't eat him. He was repugnant to me. I hated him. I loved you, Mom. I ate your heart and flesh. I thought perhaps some of your deeply hidden goodness might come to me.

I replaced the boards in our cabin, the ones where the blood dripped onto them. I scrubbed the floors. I continued to catch the school bus. I told people you were sick, Mom, and that Dad left us. People never questioned this. They knew dad was an angry and abusive man.

I did the grocery shopping, drove the car, and began to go to church. The pastor wanted to visit you, Mom. I told him you did not want visitors.

Then one day I told the pastor you died, that I buried you in the back yard. I put your bones in a box, Mom. I gave you a proper burial. We celebrated your life and death at church that Sunday. The pastor gave you a nice eulogy. People in the community brought me food. I stayed in the house the rest of my senior year until I graduated. With the community's help I applied to college and got a full-ride scholarship.

Last weekend I went hunting for the first time since I left our small town. I stayed in our vacant old house. I let Bobby Briggs, the caretaker, know I was coming and he had a fire going in the wood stove when I got there. I did not see him the entire weekend. I did not want to see anyone. That's how it is when you grow up in a small town. People mind their own business. I left Bobby a note thanking him for the fire and told him I would let him know when I was coming back.

And now once again, after eating the deer's heart on Sunday and my co-worker telling me I have too many jagged edges on Monday, I am flooded with old thoughts and feelings. I am thrust back into my old way of thinking.

I never saw it coming. I feel like killing again.

I pause, breathe, and call Forrest Jefferson, the psychologist I worked with when I first came to New York City. I leave a short message asking for an emergency appointment today. I tell him, *I'm in trouble. I need help.*

Brainwashing

The summer when I was twelve my parents, who were diplomats, got assigned to Iran. The State Department told them I couldn't go with them because it wasn't safe for children.

Mom and Dad made arrangements for me to go to Camp Laurel in Maine. Then they got a letter from the State Department saying that all the diplomat's kids were going to spend the summer at The Ranch in Idaho. My parents and I talked about it and they told the State Department that they had already made arrangements for me to go to camp in Maine. The State Department informed my parents that I was required to go to The Ranch. They sent pictures of the dining hall, theater, and cabins. It looked good, so my parents did not continue to fight the order, although they were concerned. They knew something was amiss. We worked out a system so I could get in touch with them if I needed to.

On the long bus drive into The Ranch we left behind all traces of cities and civilization. When we turned onto a dirt road in the Sawtooth Mountains I saw three golden eagles which made me happy. When we got to The Ranch gate I knew I was not at a typical summer camp. There was a guard at the gate whose badge read *No Name*. The property was surrounded by barbed wire just like a maximum security prison. The staff at The Ranch searched my luggage the first day I got there. They didn't find the money in the secret compartment of my suitcase or the thin money belt I wore with my passport in it.

So there we were, a bunch of rich kids whose parents were overseas with assignments in various countries doing God knows what, to supposedly benefit The Third World. And we were at this camp in Idaho, not allowed to leave the grounds. Sometimes I'd see a car drive up to the gate. If they weren't delivering a kid, *No Name* would turn them away. One time I watched a man get out, take pictures, and talk to *No Name*.

I liked *No Name*. He was young and straight-laced, a typical military guy with a buzz-cut and a gun. Sometimes I'd go and shoot the shit with him. He was real, a down-to-earth guy from Missouri, the Show Me State.

I didn't like most of the entitled rich kids. My folks didn't raise me like that. Wherever we lived I went to local schools, learned the language, and was just another bozo on the bus. I liked being part of the herd.

In the classes The Ranch instructors tried to instill certain thoughts and ideas in our minds. We watched movies about Nazis, Mussolini, and other dictators. We listened to lectures about drug cartels in South America. The teachers assigned books to read that supported one perspective, the benefits of living in a military state. In the papers they assigned we needed to support that militaristic perspective. The library was not a typical library. The information there was limited to one worldview. We did psychodrama that supported that one position.

We were systematically being brainwashed. We were not given any of the letters that our parents sent us. I began to wonder if I would ever see my parents again. Even though I did not believe what I was being taught, I was twelve and began to have difficulty holding onto what I really did believe.

I will say this for the camp officials, they let us roam The Ranch freely as long as we stayed within the barbed wire fence. This is what saved me. Even though the wide expanses initially scared me because I was used to living in cities in America and throughout the world, I found a kind of solace in being able to wander the remote land.

Bob and I shared a room and we began exploring the land together. He was more comfortable than me wandering the vast open spaces. He had lived in Maine with his aunt and uncle when his parents were assigned overseas and had spent a lot of time in the woods. I felt safe exploring with him. One day we found a remote, pristine lake that we swam in. We talked some, but mostly we hiked in silence.

I thought I was in the middle of nowhere until Bob and I found a mining tunnel in a broken-down-outbuilding that took us off The Ranch grounds. That day we found a small town with a tiny post office. When we walked in I talked to Margaret, the elderly postmistress. I told her I was scared. I did not tell her I was being infused with information that I did not believe was true. I told her I needed to get in touch with my parents. I sent them a short telegram. I used Chunk, our code name. Then I waited. Bob's parents did not have a plan for him. They must have been more accepting that The Ranch was a normal summer camp. But Bob was my friend, and I wasn't leaving him behind. When I got a response from my parents, it said, *Go Now*.

Margaret asked Bob and me if we wanted to spend the night at her house and told us she could take us to the Greyhound Bus Station the next day. I told her I needed to leave now. She looked me right in the eyes and then she called her son who showed up in an old blue Ford pick-up. I thanked her. He took Bob and me to Boise. I got on a plane to Southern California where my Uncle Pat lived. Bob flew to Maine. I never saw him again, but heard through the grapevine that The Ranch officials found him, and he was shipped back to The Ranch. They never found me.

When the State Department informed my parents I was missing a few weeks after I escaped from The Ranch, my folks returned to the States. Iran was their last diplomatic assignment. They could no longer support a system that was brainwashing young people. My parents moved to a small western town in Arizona. They taught in the local college and we lived a simple, normal life.

My experience at The Ranch led me to become a clinical psychologist. I specialize in working with childhood and adolescent trauma. I have a private practice in New York City.

When I get Benjamin Stoller's voicemail, I hear the panic in his voice and immediately call him back.

His Muse

Jason's Muse sits quietly and patiently in the corridor. Then She moves and waits in the wings. His Muse comes in the middle of the night, at 3:13 a.m., and tries to catch his attention, but he sleeps dead. He does not awaken for his dreams and has no need to use the bathroom. He doesn't know She waits for him to awaken so he can write.

She knows his sleep of the dead is black and blank and deep and dark. It is nothingness. He doesn't have to be a dead man forever. It has been a long time since he felt alive.

Then Jason gets a call from his mother and goes home for his father's funeral. During the day he and his mother spend time drinking tea and talking at the kitchen table. They share memories of his father and begin to sort through his father's belongings. When his mother goes to bed Jason stays up late reading and writing.

He finds boxes of his writing in the closet in his childhood bedroom. He'd forgotten about those times as a boy when he sat alone by Crickly's Creek, a tributary of the Black Thrush River, and then with Benjamin Stoller. Jason remembers the day they touched each other and made each other come, the ecstasy, shame, and how they were afraid to look at each other on Monday. He wanted more. Benjamin avoided him.

Jason kept visiting the creek hoping Benjamin would show up. Benjamin did not return to Crickly's Creek, at least not when he was there. Jason lost weight. He did not sleep well. He awoke every night at 3:13 a.m. He masturbated, fantasized, and cried. He wrote poems and stories. His mother worried about him and wondered what happened.

His father told her, *Jason's in love.*

With who? she asked.

I have no idea, but he's in love.

There were no words spoken between the parents and their son. His family did not express feeling via the spoken word. His mother did make sure he had healthy food to eat and brought him glasses of freshly-squeezed orange juice.

The father told the mother, *He's writing. That's a good thing. This will pass. He is working it out.*

And he did. When Jason went away to college he took another lover and they could not keep their hands off each other. They had mutual love, lust, and long sleepless nights of passion, sucking, and pushing. He loved feeling his lovers' ripply-muscled-back and the strength of his loins. He wrote and wrote. His Muse came when he was having sex and was open.

His lover went overseas in their junior year. He thought they would last, that their love was strong enough, but that did not happen. When he wanted to visit, his lover said, *No. It's not a good idea. I've found a new man. I'm staying in France.* Jason was heart-broken and became withdrawn.

During that period of grief His Muse came, and Jason wrote prolifically. Then he graduated, got a good-paying job, and gradually stopped hearing His Muse. She came at 3:13 a.m., but he could not hear her--too much alcohol, drugs, and random sex. Once again, the sleep of the dead was upon him. Jason felt himself being passed by.

After his father's funeral Jason stays three weeks with his mother in his childhood home. He is grateful to be here. Returning to his childhood home opens him up. He recognizes the importance of His Muse's arrival at 3:13 every morning and wonders how he can nurture that relationship so he can continue to stay awake and alive. He stops drinking and using drugs.

Before Jason leaves, He tells his mother he will see her in a month. He plans to call her every day. He hates to see her suffering.

Soon after Jason returns, he meets Peter Sullivan, a professional singer. They begin dating. He hopes they will build a life together. His Muse comes every night at 3:13 a.m., and Jason writes every time. He does not forget His Muse this time.

In The Middle Of The Rotunda

I watch a man take off his clothes in the middle of the rotunda and begin to sing. He is stark naked. I stop. Other people stop, too. He has an amazing body and a beautiful tenor voice that I cannot walk away from. What is he doing here singing naked at 6 a.m. on a Monday morning with people streaming in and out, up and down, and all around?

This place is usually busy and noisy, yet no one moves. Even the security guard, a tough guy, a no-nonsense-guy, a guy who doesn't like or appreciate rule-benders, does not move as this man stands naked, singing his heart out, melodious, mystical, haunting music. I watch people's faces. They are mesmerized. I am mesmerized, too, here in this rotunda where the Fresco of Angels is high above us.

Still no one moves. After thirty minutes, the man puts his clothes on, singing all the while. When he bows his head, it is like we are all in church.

Afterwards, I watch the singer stand in the middle of the rotunda as people flow around him. Some people stand at the edges, but I have to go up to him. In our conversation I learn he is Peter Sullivan, a professional singer who watched his mother die the day before. He is honoring her final request to sing in this rotunda, to let the angels hear his voice call to attention the spirits of those living and now dead. Her last words to Peter were, *Sing naked in the rotunda, my son, for me, for all the souls that need to be saved.*

The voice inside my head says, *Does my soul need to be saved? Save me!*

I blow off work that day. I call in and tell my boss about the guy singing.

He says, "I heard about him. Every person I have talked to has been personally touched. See you tomorrow, Jason. Make good use of your day."

And I do.

I ask Peter, "Can I take you to breakfast?"

I am in my grey striped Armani suit, and he is a lot more casual in blue jeans, a black wool sports coat, and functional shoes, perfect for this cold, wet, New York City November. I feel an immediate attraction. He looks me up and down, and I must have passed some test.

"Yes," he says.

"Let's go to Johny's Luncheonette," I say.

He nods. He knows the place. I get it right, one gay man to another. We do not make small talk as we walk in sync in the soft rain. We both are breathless when we get to the café. Johny looks at us and smiles.

"I didn't know you guys knew each other."

We both smile at Johny and give a little nod. We begin the conversation that has not stopped over the past sixteen years.

Juncko

Juncko leaves Waverly, her family estate, and looks back at the tall windows that frame the thick oak door decorated with the Christmas wreath that has three aluminum bells and a big red ribbon. Christmas is long gone. It is a hot, muggy July morning. Juncko usually avoids looking at the window on the second floor above the door because she knows there's a chance that her mother, Rita, will be watching from the window, standing with her palms pressed flat on the glass, her mouth screwed up tight.

Juncko does not like seeing her mother like that, and she does not like feeling guilty when she leaves. This time, though, when she turns, her mother stands at the window smiling. Their eyes meet. Juncko waves, and her mother puts one hand on the glass while she holds the book Juncko gave her in the other hand.

Since she was ten years old, Juncko has not lived at Waverly, the red-brick mansion that has been in her family for generations. Juncko's mother, grandmother, and great grandmother grew up here. Juncko is next in line to inherit Waverly, but she does not want this monstrous house with its empty, mausoleum-like rooms and windows that beckon from behind lace curtains. People cannot see in through the lace, yet those inside, see everything. Juncko gave up watching long ago.

When Juncko was seven years old, she remembers waiting with her mother on the front stoop of Camille Loretta Martin's house at 475 McKinley Place. Rita asked Camille Loretta, called CL, if she would take care of Juncko for a few days and CL agreed. Rita saw CL as non-threatening. She trusted her because she was a single, quiet, mousey-looking woman who wore many layers of clothes to make herself appear overweight. CL did not want people to see her small, athletic frame and her short, blond, curly hair that she covered with one of her many hats. CL Martin was not who she appeared to be.

When CL opened her red door that first time, seven-year-old Juncko and CL sized each other up. When their eyes met, Juncko felt her heart beat faster. She knew something good could happen. CL did not let Juncko's mother enter her red door that day, or any day. Juncko felt hope.

CL's door was decorated with a simple pine Christmas wreath. There was no red bow or bells, but there was a silvery sheen that Juncko was immediately drawn to. When she looked more closely, she saw hundreds of tiny, silver, tear-drop bells surrounding the wreath that she hadn't noticed.

After going through the red door, CL took Juncko to a large, high-ceilinged, round room with floor-to-ceiling windows and a table that nearly filled the entire room. The room was full of books and art supplies. Juncko had never seen an artist's studio like this. She waited at the door, afraid to enter the space. CL stood quietly next to her.

It is the quiet that Juncko remembers so clearly. It is the quiet that she came to love and appreciate. But more than the quiet, it was the opportunity that CL offered her. That day, Rita, unknowingly, gave Juncko her escape from her life at Waverly.

Juncko was a quiet, artistic girl who hated her mother's flamboyant ways and learned early the advantages of staying in the background. There was nothing subtle about Rita. When she was out wandering the streets of The City she wore big capes and bold hats. She wanted to make a statement and draw attention to herself, but inside Waverly, Rita was withdrawn and paranoid.

That first time Juncko stayed at CL's for a week. She spent most of her time with CL in the round, glass room making a mobile that has hung in that room for years. Later, CL commissioned a metal artist to make a replica of Juncko's mobile that hangs outside by the pond. It is CL's tribute to Juncko, this girl that CL loves, her daughter, not by birth, but by choice.

Juncko was not supposed to be at CL's for a week but Rita lost track of time. CL gave Juncko a room on the second floor that looked out at Central Park. It was a cozy room that had its own bathroom and a striped green bedspread with matching curtains that were always tied back. As Juncko grew older and made the room her own, she took down the curtains. Juncko liked light coming in.

When CL came into Juncko's life, Juncko did not want to lose her. She missed having a mother who could take care of her. As Rita wandered around The City more frequently, she left her daughter with CL more often. Two weeks after her first visit, when Juncko saw CL at the corner market, Juncko knew she loved CL

Martin. Juncko was careful to not show any enthusiasm or excitement when she was going to CL's.

Juncko remembered back to being excited after her first day of kindergarten. Marilla, her nanny since the day she was born, picked her up, and Juncko chattered all the way home. When they walked in the door, Juncko was laughing and called Marilla *mama*. Rita began screaming and told Marilla to get out, that Juncko already had a mother and it was not Marilla. Marilla tried to reason with Rita, but she pushed Marilla and slapped her. Juncko called Mr. Brewster, the manager of the estate, who had taken it upon himself to protect her and Rita. He tried to reason with Rita, but she did not listen. Juncko was devastated. She cried quietly when Marilla walked out the door. She blamed herself for Marilla being fired because she knew she was not supposed to call her *mama*. It had slipped out in the excitement of her telling Rita about her first day at school.

Juncko had difficulty sleeping after Marilla left. She had to pick out her own clothes to wear and when she asked her mother to help her with her reading log, her mother could not focus enough to do it. The truth is, Rita had never been much of a mother. She was not able to care for herself, let alone, a small child. Mr. Brewster helped take care of Juncko until CL came into the picture.

When Juncko turned ten CL talked to Mr. Brewster about getting Rita's permission to take Juncko out of public school and enroll her in a private school for creative children. CL and Juncko took the subway to meet Mr. Brewster and discuss the school change and the possibility of Juncko living full-time with CL. CL took Juncko to Johny's Luncheonette, the only diner in New York City that had baklava made to her satisfaction.

Juncko had never been on the subway before. She and Rita walked everywhere or took cabs. CL was a wealthy woman, yet she believed that every New Yorker should know the subway system. She and Juncko explored the entire city by taking the subway so Juncko could get around The City by herself. CL believed that being 'of the people' was important, and joining in the richness of cultures was integral to a child's growth. They went to the Metropolitan Museum of Modern Art, the Guggenheim, and wandered around Central Park where Juncko had her first ride on the merry-go-round. She loved it. They took the boat and climbed up the stairs in the

Statue of Liberty. Exploring The City had been part of CL's education when she was a child and she wanted that for Juncko.

Not only did Mr. Brewster help with Juncko changing schools, he successfully got Rita to sign over her parental rights to CL. Mr. Brewster, his father, and his grandfather had been managing her family's estate for decades. He paid the taxes and made sure that Rita had a stable living arrangement. When Rita got pregnant as a single woman, Mr. Brewster helped her get pre-natal care. He also made sure Juncko was taken care of after she was born.

Rita willingly signed the papers that gave control of her daughter's life and destiny to CL. Rita did not explain to her daughter why she was giving her up, but Rita did tell Juncko she wanted the best for her. Juncko knew Rita was not stupid. She wondered if her mother knew she was mentally ill.

By this time Rita was spending more and more time wandering around The City. She lost weight and had trouble remembering she even had a daughter. As time went on Rita was unable to find her way back to Waverly without assistance from the police. Her mental illness was progressing, and she was either completely silent or she could not stop talking. CL tried to get help for Rita but Rita refused to be confined or take medication.

Juncko went home to Waverly to get her things. CL waited outside. Mr. Brewster kept Rita occupied. His instruction to Juncko was to take whatever she wanted from her room. Juncko went upstairs by herself and pulled out her suitcases from the closet. She filled them with books and the old glass bells that her grandfather had gotten on a trip to Italy. These thirteen Murano glass bells had hung over Juncko's baby crib and later by the window when she was a small girl. While she was packing, Juncko could hear her mother's loud voice intermingled with Mr. Brewster's quiet one.

Juncko thrived living with CL. CL invited Marilla to come back into Juncko's life. Marilla told CL, *I'm so glad you called me. I was devastated when Rita kicked me out and banned me from Juncko's life. I love Juncko. She was like my daughter. We spent every day of the first five years of her life together. I was so worried about her when I had to leave that day. Don't get me wrong, Rita loves Juncko, but she wasn't able to take care of her. I stayed in touch with Mr. Brewster and I'm really happy that you're her legal guardian. I am glad I can be back in her life again.*

CL was thrilled that Marilla wanted to support Juncko.

Once a month, from the time Juncko was ten years old, until she graduated from high school, Juncko and CL had dinner with Rita, when she was well enough.

When Juncko was twenty-five she wrote her first book, *The Swallow*, and published it under a pseudonym to protect her mother. Juncko wanted to dedicate the book to CL. CL asked Juncko to think about the dedication and Juncko ended up dedicating the book, *to all my mothers, Rita, CL, Marilla, and Mr. B.*

Juncko gave her mother a copy of her book. By this time Rita was confused and unable to speak in complete sentences. Mr. Brewster had hired a live-in caregiver.

A month later, Rita wandered out of Waverly and was found dead in an alley. Juncko kept thinking about the last time she saw Rita. She was glad she had turned around and saw her mother's smiling face with her book in her hand.

After the funeral, Juncko began cleaning out Waverly so she could sell it. She found a newspaper article in a wooden sewing box in her mother's closet. The article read, *Two years ago, sixteen year old Rita Marie Weller was gang-raped a few months after her parents died in a plane crash. No one was ever apprehended for the rape. Now, an unnamed witness has come forward to say he has the identities of the rapists. Rita got pregnant from the attack. During her pregnancy she was confined to The Pink Palace, a mental institution, where she carried her baby to term. At first her behavior was thought to be trauma from the rape. Later she was diagnosed with schizophrenia.*

Juncko called CL and Mr. Brewster after reading the article. Mr. Brewster told Juncko that Rita's family was ill-equipped to deal with a grieving teen who had lost her parents. When she got pregnant, the family was so overwhelmed they asked him to manage the situation. He hired Doris Kelleher to take care of Rita during her pregnancy. Doris protected Rita, but she couldn't stop her from wandering the city streets. What no one knew at the time was that Rita had been gang-raped by five young men who held her down and taped her mouth. Rita never talked about what happened that night. She continued wandering around The City, often ending up where her rape occurred.

Juncko cried as she listened to Mr. Brewster. He put his arm around her and comforted her. CL sat next to her, held her hand, and cried, too. Juncko talked about how she wished she had been able to talk to her mother about the loss of her parents and the rape. Juncko wondered if she could have helped her mother break through her pain and suffering. Mr. Brewster and CL listened to Juncko and told her they did not feel that Rita would have been helped by being reminded of the death of her parents or the rape. These were painful losses and Rita did not handle loss well.

Juncko asked questions that Mr. Brewster could not adequately answer. He recommended Juncko contact Ray Olson, the attorney she met at Rita's funeral. Mr. Brewster believed Ray could tell her more about Rita. Juncko called Ray Olson and left a message.

One afternoon when Juncko was cleaning out Waverly the doorbell rang. She was expecting the realtor, but when she looked out the window with the lace curtains that hid her from view, she saw Mr. Olson standing on the porch. Juncko ran downstairs and let him in.

Mr. Olson told Juncko, "I was the attorney who worked with Clancy Lawrence, the detective who dealt with cold cases. When Clancy saw my photos of the men who brutally gang-raped your mother, he knew he had information that would get them convicted. I caught these men on camera and developed the pictures. I was around the same age as those men when the rape occurred. I wanted to get those men. I bided my time. While I was in law school I researched the process and learned the New York statutes.

By the time Bobby Briggs turned twenty-one, all five men were married and all but Bobby had children. Bobby did not rape your mother, but he held her down while the others did. He got out of prison in five years. I didn't care that these men had families. I didn't care that their wives would be devastated. I only cared about helping your mother and you and bringing the case to justice.

Your mother was not a witness and did not attend the trial. At the trial, the police report and my graphic photographs sealed their fate. The five men accused were convicted."

After Ray Olson left, Juncko realized she does not want to sell Waverly. She wants to be in her family home and write the story of Rita's life. She wants to find and interview Bobby Briggs and the four men in prison. She wants to find her father.

The St. Lawrence

The Pink Palace

I find the book in the patient library behind some larger books. I read all evening and late into the night. I cannot put down Lise Straub's book about Roxanne and The Pink Palace. I get the feeling someone hid it there. I don't think the staff would want us patients to read it.

Roxanne came from a wealthy family. Her father was a physician, and her mother was from a prosperous, southern plantation-owning family. Roxanne met Simon at a Christmas party at her parents' house. It was love at first sight for Simon, but Roxanne played hard to get. They got married after a short courtship, but on their honeymoon Simon experienced Roxanne's severe mood swings. He thought he could manage them by building The Pink Palace, a large house on one of the 1000 Islands in the St. Lawrence River. You needed a boat to get to it, except in the winter when The River would freeze and you could walk across the thick ice.

At first Roxanne loved The Pink Palace, even though being there did not alleviate her mood swings. During Roxanne's first winter there she grew isolated and unhappy. She often sat naked, staring out the second story window at the icicles as the sun's light made rainbows. When Simon arrived home from work one afternoon he discovered his naked wife masturbating and humming an eerie tune that he found particularly disconcerting. He told the housekeeper to help Roxanne get dressed every day so she would be less inclined to spend her time masturbating.

Roxanne's friends came to lunch regularly and one of the men always stayed for three to four hours of after-lunch activities in Roxanne's bedroom to help satisfy her insatiable sexual appetite. Then all the men stopped coming around, except Daniel, who came by canoe two days a week. Simon did not know about him.

Simon and Roxanne did not have children. He became frustrated with her inability to conceive his child. Roxanne left The Pink Palace pregnant with Daniel's child and moved to a small cottage on a lake a hundred miles away. She had a daughter who they named Bethesda May Ceres. Roxanne, now Roxy, was known as The Rainbow Lady because she hung crystal prisms all around the exterior of their house.

Simon was heartbroken after Roxy disappeared. He never discovered his wife's whereabouts. He eventually left the area and sold The Pink Palace to the state who turned it into a mental hospital. They built a bridge connecting the island to the mainland to make access easier.

I put down Lise Straub's book when I read about the mental hospital and the bridge. I remember the day Tom and Sharon, my brother and sister-in-law, drove me to The Pink Palace. The place seemed welcoming with the pink crystals surrounding the glass façade entrance. I couldn't stop looking at the rainbows. I felt crazy and was not functioning well.

I had a break when my two-year old daughter, Carmella Stone, died. I kept seeing her dead body floating in the pond near my house. I have to hand it to Tom and Sharon, they checked on me at home for a long time, but eventually I couldn't be left alone. I wasn't safe. I became childlike. I felt guilty about my daughter's death, yet all the guilt in the world wasn't bringing her back.

My husband died in a car crash two weeks after I gave birth to Carmella. I guess the grief finally got to me. I could not get out of bed in the morning even after sixteen hours of sleep. I stopped going to work and lost my job. I stopped taking showers. I was never hungry. I lost forty pounds. I was skin and bones. I thought a lot about dying. I had no daughter. I had no husband. I understood that Tom and Sharon had no choice. I know they loved me.

I vaguely remember Sharon researching places where I might get help. She found The Pink Palace and knew I would like being on the St. Lawrence River. When she found out they had an opening, we drove up there that day.

Outsiders do not see the rooms. They are individual cells with high windows and bars. My hand is small so my fingers and hand can fit through the bars. I can pass a piece of paper or a small glass through the bars, but not anything large. It's how I get a letter out. I write it and drop it out the window, hoping the wind will carry my message away. Destination unknown. I hope someone will find it.

I ask for help. I have been here too long. I see the effect that being here has, not only on me, but on all the patients. There is a deadness with intermittent screams during the night, followed by the swishing of guards and the opening of the iron doors whereupon the screaming subsides.

I see Dr. Barnes three times a week, Theodore Barnes, MD, PhD from Harvard, a brilliant man, yet I am trying to get over on him. That is not easy to do. He seems to know all the games.

Lydia, another patient, gives me the scoop my third month here. "Follow the program. Cheek the meds. They'll be the death of you. Tell Dr. Barnes what he wants to hear."

At the time I don't know what he wants to hear.

Lydia says, "You'll know. Pay attention. Get on his good side. He'll release you eventually."

After six months, when Lydia and I are working in the laundry room, I tell her, "I need to get out. I don't want to live in The Pink Palace for the rest of my life."

Lydia nods. She tells me stories of patients who get put in an outbuilding on the property, are chained to beds, and are subdued with medication.

"In effect, they are prisoners," she says.

I don't want to believe that.

One night I hear two nurses talking about Rita, a pregnant woman who was discharged. We had a party for her. Rita was vocal about patient rights. Her estate manager, Mr. Brewster came to see her every month. She had a discharge date. When a third nurse arrives, she asks me what I'm doing outside the nurses' station. I slink back to my room.

I've been here a year now. Sharon and Tom visit me once a month. I have worked hard with Dr. Barnes, and he and I are talking about my discharge plan. But I have a queasy feeling in my gut that tells me leaving here is not going to be easy.

As I continue to read Lise Straub's book I find out that Roxanne got put in The Pink Palace after Daniel died. She went crazy. In one of her letters to Bethesda, Roxanne talks about knowing she's never going to get out of The Pink Palace and begs her daughter to get her out. They never release her. Roxanne drowns while swimming to the shore.

Straub ends her book writing about the tragedy of Roxanne's life and the abuse of power by mental health professionals. I came here voluntarily. I am ready to leave. I will advocate for myself in my next session with Dr. Barnes. I will firm up my discharge date. I am done biding my time. If I am the prisoner I think I am, I will plan my escape, for me, for Roxy, and for all the sensitive ones.

I will write a letter to Lise Straub and ask Sharon and Tom to mail it for me. Maybe Lise can help me. If all else fails, I will wait until summer when the water is less cold and do what Roxanne failed to do. I am a good swimmer. I believe I can make it to the mainland.

Hatching A Plan

Three years ago Maria left New York City and moved to the small town of Cape Vincent, whose claim to fame is being where Lake Ontario and the St. Lawrence River meet. She moved here for three reasons. One, she was fascinated by, and wanted to discover exactly where, these two large bodies of water came together. Two, she wanted to be part of Cape Vincent's strong women's community, and three, she loved the small-town library.

Maria loves living here. Cape Vincent is home.

Maria has been in a relationship with Nancy for the past two years. Maria is tired of their fights and her never-ending concessions where she gives up her power, loses her voice, and feels like a victim. On Saturday night when Nancy picks another fight, Maria reacts, and Nancy walks out. Maria is alone again. As she sits on the couch eating popcorn and watching *Arsenic and Old Lace,* she begins to hatch a plan to get out of her relationship with Nancy.

Many women in her community believe Nancy Newhouse is evil, but no one has been willing to do anything about it. Nancy has used and abused a string of women who left Cape Vincent after she broke up with them. Maria will find and talk with Nancy's ex-partners. She will gather information. Maria starts with Nancy's most recent ex-lover, Trudi. They meet at Johny's Luncheonette in Manhattan.

Trudi tells Maria, "After I left Cape Vincent it took me two long years to get my head on straight. I took a bus to New York City so I could escape into the abyss of sounds and endless people. I needed to be anonymous. I got hurt really badly by Nancy and felt like I had to do a physical move to survive. I know this sounds dramatic, but that's how it was for me. When Nancy and I got together, Nancy's ex-lover, Sally, was a train wreck. I didn't think Nancy would treat me like she did Sally. I was naïve and foolish. People are the same, no matter who they're with. Just because Sally and I were both athletic, fit, well-read, and educated, didn't stop us from being vulnerable to *out-there-in-your-face* Nancy, bold, aggressive, sexy, *making-you-feel-like-a-million-bucks* Nancy. She's the quintessential extrovert, always picking the introvert. But it was the incredibly passionate and persistent sex that was the hook for me.

Kinky in a good way, an aphrodisiac. Nancy's body was incredible, and she has great hands and fingers." She smiles and adds, "Important assets for a lesbian."

Maria smiles back and says, "Ain't that the truth."

Then Maria finds Sally.

"I had twenty-five years sober when I met Nancy." Sally stops and stares out the window. "I'm a month sober now. It's been rough. I've got a good sponsor now though, and I just moved into a sober-living house with five other women. I'm beginning to see the light."

Maria asks, "What happened?

"I got caught in Nancy's web. She was like a drug to me. I couldn't stay away from her. I couldn't get enough of the sex. It was hypnotic. As I got more dependent on the intense sex, I started to drink again, and then I got lost. I lost my job, lost myself, and ultimately, I lost Nancy. She told me I was a burden to her and started dating Trudi. I had to leave Cape Vincent. I was in so much pain. I couldn't stand seeing her with another woman. And I couldn't stop drinking."

Maria sighs and nods.

Babs was the most disturbing casualty. Maria met first with Bab's mother who showed her pictures of Babs in high school and college. She was a normal, beautiful, vivacious young woman, and now it was unlikely she would ever come out of her psychotic state. Her mother hated Nancy. Maria told Bab's mother that she was gathering information about Nancy so she could write an article. Bab's mother gave Maria permission to visit her daughter in the mental hospital, The Pink Palace.

When Maria enters Bab's room she says, "I'm Maria. I live in Cape Vincent."

Babs immediately begins talking non-stop about Nancy and sex. She cries and takes Maria's hand and puts it on her breast. When Maria withdraws her hand, Babs takes her own hand, puts it on her crotch, and begins to masturbate. Maria watches in fascination, and then with horror, as Babs yells Nancy's name louder and louder until she comes. One of the attendants arrives during the incident and ends Maria's visit. Maria leaves, horrified.

Like Trudi, Sally, and Babs, Maria has found it difficult to take care of herself during and after sex with Nancy, however, Maria has not lost herself. She is attractive, well educated, physically fit, and has a good job, just like the other women, but Maria's blue-collar roots make her different. She has witnessed child abuse, sexual abuse, drug deals, and down-and-dirty addiction. Maria has a tough underbelly and a place in her heart that no one has ever touched.

Maria doubts that it is only these three women's lives that Nancy has destroyed. Maria continues her mission to gather information about Nancy so she can write an article and expose her.

A week later Maria finds herself alone in Nancy's apartment when Nancy gets called in early to work. Maria gets her first chance to snoop around. She finds an envelope addressed to Nancy Needicks, which is not the last name Nancy uses now. The return address is L. Fletcher, 1652 Wild Horse Lane in Bluffton, South Carolina. Maria finds no letter, only the envelope. In the back of Nancy's underwear drawer Maria finds a small faded envelope with a man's watch with *To RF* engraved on the back of it, a class ring from Bluffton High School, one earring with a blue stone, a small black and white photo of an attractive older woman, a silver Celtic cross with a broken chain, and a man's small white handkerchief with the letters NN embroidered on it.

When Maria gets home she calls information, gets the phone number, and calls L. Fletcher. The Voicemail says, *This is Lynette Fletcher. You know what to do. I'll get back to you as soon as possible.* Maria leaves a message.

Good afternoon. My name is Toni Matthews. I'm writing an article on Nancy Needicks and have heard that you may be able to help me. I'd appreciate it if you would call me back.

Three hours later Lynette calls back. Maria lets the call go to voicemail, so she can hear Lynette's voice. Lynette sounds nervous. Maria is anxious too. Before she calls her back, Maria makes a cup of peppermint tea, sits down at her kitchen table with a notebook and pen so she can take notes, and takes out her recently purchased disposable phone.

Twenty minutes later Maria phones Lynette. Maria says, "I'm gathering background information on Nancy Needicks for a magazine article I've been commissioned to write."

Lynette says, "I can help you." After a brief pause she launches into her story. "Nancy and I grew up in Bluffton. It's a small town right on the Intracoastal Waterway. We went all the way from kindergarten to high school together. We were both poor, but Nancy was smart and got a scholarship to Harvard."

Maria asks, "What about her family?"

Lynette says, "Nancy's parents died in a car crash right after she got accepted to Harvard. Tragic accident. They went off the road and slammed into a tree. No one knows why."

Maria asks, "What are her parent's names?"

"Marjorie and Norman Needicks. Nancy wrote their obituary for our local paper. The whole town showed up for their funeral that day. It was a really hot summer day. I remember cuz we were all sweatin' and everybody was cryin'. We all felt sorry for Nancy, but she's a trooper. She didn't cry. A few weeks later, before she left for college, she put her brother in a private care facility. He lived at home all those years with a brain injury he got when he was little." Lynette pauses and takes a breath. "Nancy went on like it was business as usual."

Maria waits, then asks, "What happened to her brother?"

Lynette says matter-of-factly, "Well, there's two stories. One is that he fell off the slide at the park and banged his head hard on the concrete. The other is that Nancy dropped him."

During that silence, Char, Lynette's partner, gets on the phone with Maria and says, "I'm worried about Lynette's safety. Nancy's a crazy mother-fucker."

Maria reassures Char and tells her, "I'm using a non-traceable disposable phone."

"That might be the ticket," says Char. "I don't want my girl gettin' hurt."

Maria likes that Char is protective of Lynette.

Maria learns that Lynette is loyal to Nancy and that they were lovers in high school.

"I know I'm not one of those smart, well-dressed babes that Nancy likes now, but I've stuck by her all these years. She trusts me to take care of her brother who's in a real nice care home now in Charleston. I pay his bills and visit him every Wednesday. I make sure they're treatin' him right."

And then Maria gets her first break, a crack in the loyalty armor.

116

"Nancy doesn't know I'm with Char. When she comes to town, Char leaves for a couple of days and accepts that I'm gonna do Nancy because, hell, Nancy pays our way, more than pays our way. She's generous. Char and me take Olivia cruises. I have to tell Nancy when I'm goin' cuz I'll miss my weekly visit to the care home. Nancy thinks I go alone, but of course it's me and Char, has been for years. I don't really know if her knowin' about Char would change anything, but I'm not willin' to take the risk. I don't wanna rock the boat. Nancy's got a mean streak in her a mile wide."

A week later in their next conversation Lynette tells Maria, "Char got me a non-traceable disposable phone. Can you call me back on that number?"

They talk about Nancy's mean streak.

"Nancy has a long history of abusin' girls and women." Lynette's voice is low, almost a whisper. "She'll kill me if she finds out I've been talkin' to you."

There is a hushed silence that Maria does not attempt to break.

Lynette clears her throat, "You still there?"

"Yes," Maria replies softly. "I'm listening."

"I've got somethin' I need to tell you."

"I'm all ears," says Maria.

"Nancy killed PammyLyn Joseph when we were kids."

Maria repeats, "Nancy killed PammyLyn Joseph?"

"Yeah. A group of us girls went to the lake. My momma dropped us off early and we spent the day there. A friend's mom came at 5 to pick us up, but Nancy, me, and PammyLyn didn't wanna leave, so the other girls left, and that's when it happened. I was sittin' on the shore and Nancy and PammyLyn were messin' around in the water. When I came back from the bathroom I didn't see PammyLyn. Nancy claimed she didn't know where she was, but I didn't believe her. They'd been out there playin' around in deep water. PammyLyn was a good swimmer, but not as good as Nancy, and they were pretty far out. Nancy said PammyLyn just went down, but I didn't believe her. Said she swam in, and the next thing she knew PammyLyn wasn't behind her. I remember my throat tightenin' when she told me that. She also told me PammyLyn would turn up. I knew she wouldn't. I've seen Nancy bury a girl in mud before and wanna leave her there, but the rest of us girls realized she was strugglin' to breathe, so we dug her out. Nancy stood there and watched us dig. She never said a word, just smoked her cigarette and stared. That girl never went with us again. It changed her. If Nancy knew I was talkin' to you, she would have no problem killin' me."

Maria had the story she'd been looking for. Should she go to the police? What would they say? She had no evidence. Lynette broke into Maria's reverie.

"She has PammyLyn's ring."

"What?"

"She has her Bluffton High School ring. She kept it. I don't know why. She showed it to me. I felt warned, like I better keep my mouth shut. And I have. I owe her. My brother, Rodney, used to touch me. She set him straight. Held a gun to his head and told him, *I should kill you. I love your sister. If you ever touch her again, I'll find you. Your life will be over.* Rodney took her serious and stopped fuckin' with me. He died that next year in a random shooting. When I went to identify his body, they gave me his wallet. I asked about his watch, but they said he wasn't wearin' one when they brought him in. My brother always wore his watch. It had *To RF* on the back. It belonged to my grandaddy, then my daddy. When Daddy died, my brother got it. They all had the same name, Rodney Fletcher. When I told Nancy he'd been shot and killed, she didn't seem surprised, and she certainly wasn't sorry. I forgave him. Nancy never did."

At the end of that conversation, Lynette says, "I can't talk to you anymore. Even with this phone I don't feel safe."

Maria thanks her and says, "I'd like to meet with you in person after I've written the article."

Lynette is quiet. The she says, "I don't want you comin' to my house, but we might could meet at BeeBee's Diner. It's in Savannah. Let me talk to Char."

Maria says," Okay. Can I call you on the disposable phone in a couple of days to talk about meeting at BeeBee's?"

More silence followed by, "Yeah. That'll work."

After Maria hangs up she sees the colors in the sky and knows a storm is brewing. Maria realizes her article has now turned into a book, and that Nancy is a serial killer. Maria has to be careful. She takes out a clean white piece of paper and begins to write. She knows this is going to be a long night.

My Nana

I sit at my Nana's built-in desk. I love its nooks and crannies and bright green alabaster bookends shaped like a leaf. In the corner I see her cane carved with Celtic knots and a wooden mermaid on top. I'm afraid to pick up the cane.

The first time I touched the cane was the Halloween I dressed up as a mermaid. I felt a jolt of electricity that scared me. Before I dropped it, I saw images of women swimming naked in a clear blue pool of water. Some were human, some part mermaid, some full mermaid; a society of women in transformation.

Do I look like somebody who came from the sea? I asked her.

That's not the point, Summer. My Nana was always saying this.

When I got older I asked her, *What is the point?*

The point is, there's a whole world that's invisible. It's just below the surface and you have to dive deep to get to it.

Do mermaids live there? I asked.

They do. And you come from Mer-women. We both come from this Clan.

How come we left the water?

Because we have another path to follow, another purpose.

Like what? I asked her.

I don't know your path, Summer, but I knew the day you were born you were one of us. I saw it in your face. There was no stopping you from exploring the depths. Swimming in the water and diving deep is what Mer-women do. Ultimately, we find treasure. Of course, it isn't that simple, but that's the end result. In between there are barriers that can hurt, and perhaps, kill you. Yet, if you're to become the woman you're meant to be, you must journey. You must go into the fear, Summer.

What does that mean, Nana?

It means to know the fear. To struggle with the fear. Make peace with the fear and grow past the fear. Accept that the fear is real and let it become your guide.

I sit at my Nana's desk with tears streaming down my face. My heart hurts. I miss her so much. My Nana left me the cane so I can access the depths more easily. The cane is the portal to the magical worlds. I pick up the cane and feel the familiar jolt. For the first time I hold onto it because I want to journey, and know I can, if I don't drop it.

I journey alone. I have memories of journeying together with Nana as my guide. She teaches me it is not only important, but necessary, to dive into the depths. I see Nana smiling at me and laughing with the Mer-women. She lets me know I can visit her anytime. She reminds me grief is necessary, suffering is not.

I love you, Nana. I miss you.

She reaches out her hand. I reach back.

Grandad's Secret

Cam and I are driving down a dirt road when a soft rain begins. All is well, but there's a shift in the weather. The rain is no longer coming down in drops, it's coming down in sheets. The car slips and slides. It mirrors the trees that are blowing like crazy, the branches that are being torn off like unneeded limbs, and the leaves that are being shaken and ripped off. *A real nor'easter* I think, and say it to Cam, who's sitting quietly in the passenger seat. We haven't spoken since the heavy rain began. Actually, our words ended soon after we turned onto the dirt road.

"Where the fuck are you taking me, Summer?" Cam asks.

I don't respond because Cam already knows where we're going. I told him. He'd been up for the adventure. Now he seems uptight and annoyed. I neglected to tell him that the old hotel I'm looking for is on some unknown dirt road by the St. Lawrence River.

Several months ago when I was alone, driving aimlessly, I came upon an old abandoned hotel that was falling apart. I couldn't get it out of mind. I was mesmerized by the old wooden keyboard with key hooks still intact, the room numbers below the hooks. There was only one key on the board, Room 317. I had no idea where the other keys were. I had no idea where room 317 was either. The place was small. It looked to me like it couldn't have more than twenty-five rooms, if that. Yet the board had all those hooks, and there was this one lone key. I took it.

I shouldn't have taken the key. My mission is to return it. Well that's part of my mission. The other part is to find Room 317, and see if the key unlocks the door.

That first time I got to the hotel it was sunset, and I didn't have a chance to explore the place before darkness came. All the doors I tried were locked. I pushed the bell, the little half bell on the counter to let somebody know you're there. No one came. I wanted to take the half-bell and the key board, but I didn't. I only took the key.

When I got home, I showed my grandad the key. He told me he remembered old keys like this from when he was a boy and his family had stayed at an old resort on the St. Lawrence.

This was before the mills came, Summer. They took away the resorts because the mills made more money. The mills were better for the pocketbook, but they left the land a wreck. It was hard to watch. These resorts were alive with people, families mostly, although your nana and I honeymooned at one of them, The Rusty Nail, a hotel for adults; married and unmarried couples, straight, gay. They were alternative life-style places. They had great food, good conversation, comfortable beds, privacy, liquor, and the finest marijuana. You could have sex with anybody you wanted. Your nana and I liked the crowd. We didn't have sex with anybody other than each other. That was our agreement. But we did play poker and we did end up getting ourselves in some sticky situations. Your nana, as you know, was quite beautiful. Lots of men wanted her.

He looked up at me and caught my eye.

You know what I mean, Summer?

I nodded.

She was a looker, and we used that to get men to give us-no-her-money. She did things for us that I'm not proud of, you know, sexual things.

I looked at my grandad to see if he was joking around with me, but he had a far-away look in his eyes and seemed to have forgotten I was in the room.

Your nana never let other men enter her body, but she gave them hand jobs until they came, and amazingly they kept coming back for more. She had a way with these gentlemen that made them feel real important, like they mattered. When they signed up for an hour, they got an hour, a full sixty minutes. Most of the time what they wanted was somebody to listen to them. They were lonely, Summer, like you were, until you met Cam.

He was right. I had been lonely. I hated the empty feeling I went to sleep with every night. I was tired of one-night stands and meaningless sex.

So here I am with Cam, and he's pissed off or something. I don't know what's going on with him. I can think of a lot of things I could say, but it all feels like small talk. I decide against it. The point is, he's here in the car, and he hasn't said, *Turn around.* I know he won't because he isn't that kind of guy. When he agrees to do something he sticks with it, even when he doesn't want to. I admire this about him because I'm not like that at all. If I don't like something, I walk away, get the hell out of Dodge. Cam has more moral character than me, although my grandad would not necessarily have called it that. I think about my grandad talking about the alternative lifestyle resorts on the river, and I wonder if this place I'm trying to find again is one of them.

And then suddenly, I recognize the place. I see a sign that I didn't see the first time, USTY AIL.

"It must be the Rusty Nail," I say.

Cam says, "Maybe. Or it could be, Busty Bail, Crusty Tail, Lusty Mail, Gusty Sail, Musty Jail, Trusty Pail. There's a lot of possibilities, Summer."

I laugh. He laughs, too.

Cam and I find Room 317, and the key unlocks the door. I see the light shining on the river. We make love on an old mattress. I cry as I tell Cam the story my grandad told me about him and my nana. Cam holds me. I wonder if my grandparents stayed in this room with its magnificent view of the St. Lawrence. I wonder if my mother knows this story about her parents. I do not wonder if she will hear my grandad's secret from me. My lips are sealed.

New England

Piercing The Veil

I see the man holding the bloody knife. He has pierced my friend's veil and stabbed her. Her eyes get wide, and I feel her fear as I watch from the booth across the aisle. I am shocked and afraid. I see her head fall forward and touch her chest. She looks like she is praying. I know she's dead, and if I don't leave the outdoor market immediately, he will find and kill me, too.

As I stand there the woman shopkeeper pushes me deeper into her booth and points to a hidden alleyway. I look at her briefly, take a risk, and strip down to my Western clothes. She signals me to take off my veil, something I am not supposed to do. She takes my burka, puts it in a basket, and covers it with scarves. I put on my hat. I move quickly towards the alleyway.

We heard about the attacks at the all-girls school that I attend in Tehran. An American woman and a German man came to our school. They talked with each class individually instead of holding a whole school assembly. They told us they didn't want to draw attention to the school. Our teachers were scared for our safety and wanted us to be prepared. They told each of us to wear a skirt or pants, a shirt, and have a hat under our burka.

The American said, "If something happens, you need to get rid of the burka immediately and head toward the international section of the city. Blend in as much as possible. Find a phone booth and call this number."

The German said, "Some locals will help you, others will not. Always stay together. Don't separate. They will not go after two together, only a girl who is alone. That could change, but this is what is true today."

They were very matter of fact, right to the point. I hoped I'd be in less danger than most of the girls because I speak English well, but I didn't really know if this was true.

I'm shaking when I get to a phone booth. When a woman answers, I tell her, "It's Calla. I'm at Via de la Luz." Calla is the name we were told to use. Calla, like the lily, a symbol of white and light and purity. The street is still. I only hear my beating heart. Fifteen minutes later a man driving a black Mercedes pulls up. He gets out and opens the door for me. He never speaks to me. He quickly drives out of the city. I sit quietly and look out the window. As we get further away from the city center, I see children playing and hear roosters crowing. I see the driver's shoulders relax once we pass through Lux. After a while we turn off the paved road and drive down a long dirt road that ends at a large house. A woman is standing alone on the porch.

She says, "I'm Pam. You're safe here. We'll move you again in a couple of days. Let's get you a bath, and then we'll talk."

I feel my hands trembling. They are cold. I put them in my pockets.

She takes me to a sparsely furnished room that looks out at grass, trees, and a river. There's a picture of praying hands on the wall.

Smiling, she tells me, "Bathroom's down the hall on the right. Put your clothes in a pile by the door and put on the clothes that are hanging on the back of the door."

Half an hour later I join her at the table where a woman named Zahraa serves us food. She speaks to me in Persian and I respond. She assures me that Pam is a good person and I'm safe here. Zahraa leaves the room and I'm alone with Pam. I'm grateful to be here and I'm scared. My mind moves quickly from thought to thought.

Pam gently asks me, "What happened?

I say, "My friend and I were poking around the market together. She wandered across the aisle to look at something in another booth. She was there for less than a minute when I saw a man holding a knife to her throat. We were separated only briefly. I don't know if he even knew we were together. A shopkeeper saw the whole thing. She knew exactly what was happening. She helped me remove my burka and get down to my western clothes. She nodded towards the hidden alley and I slipped out into the streets, transformed into a foreigner. I called you and made my way here."

When I finish, Pam says, "The shopkeeper took a big risk. That man is with a radical Muslim group whose mission is to kill all girls who are being educated. They believe a woman's job is breeding. Part of our team is a group of mostly uneducated shopkeepers, women who do not want any young Iranian women to die. You were lucky that the shopkeeper is part of our group."

Pam continues, "I don't know when you'll be able to contact your parents. When you're safely out of Iran, someone from this agency will call your parents and tell them you're alive. They won't know where you're living until later. The group killing girls has the names and ages of all the girls in the city that are enrolled in school. They are going door to door looking for them."

I sit completely still, tears run down my face. My parents and I talked about what might happen. They knew I might be taken. *We love you*, they told me. *You need to go wherever you are sent, and God willing, we will find you and be reunited in the future.*

I never thought it would happen. And now, here I am at a safe house. I can't believe I won't see my mom, dad, and little brothers tonight. My stomach hurts and I can't stop seeing the fear in my friend's eyes. I feel guilty because I didn't stop her from going across the aisle. I can't believe my friend is dead and I have to leave.

Two days later a man posing as my husband comes for me in a small foreign car. Pam cut my hair short and dyed it blonde. I'm wearing yellow pants, an orange and white striped tunic, and sunglasses. Pam slips a wedding ring on my finger. She hugs me and touches my cheek. She hands me an American passport with the name Natalie Poland stamped on it. My newly acquired husband's name is Mark Poland. We're here on holiday. I'm an artist. In a colorful beach bag I have a sketch book and paint. On the back seat of the car I have paintings and my hands are stained with oil paint. Mark reminds me to breathe. When I look at myself in the mirror, I see almost no reminder of me. My sad brown eyes tell a different story. We're crossing into Turkey today.

At the border the men look disinterested. It is a fairly quick process. I pretend I don't understand what they're saying. Pam and Mark talked to me about this. *No recognition, they said. Don't get out of the car even if they order it. Only get out if they open your door. Then and only then.*

The men shout for us to get out of the car. I sit there making sure my hands are not clenched while they look at our papers and Mark's business credentials. They question him about what we're doing here. Mark tells them he was here on business and his wife came with him to paint. He points to the canvasses on the backseat. The men look at my stained hands resting in my lap. They stamp the papers. Mark thanks them in Farsi. We drive across the border. I sit quietly. I'm still afraid. Mark reassures me during the five-hour drive to the airport.

Mark says, "You did great. Next, you'll get on a plane for New York, and Marsha Malone will be waiting for you when you arrive. She'll take you to her house in Maine. I don't know how long you'll stay with her. You'll have to be moved at least one more time. You are not to tell anyone your real name. I don't know if you will ever be able to use your birth name again. One of the other girls we relocated to the United States disappeared when she used her Iranian name."

I am silent.

Then he says, "You're one of the lucky ones."

I look at him and nod. I know it's true, but it doesn't feel like it.

"One of your classmates was not so lucky. She made a mistake by opening the door when they were yelling at her in Farsi. They signed the American driver's papers and told him to get out of their country. The last image he had was of the girl being led away with a noose around her neck."

While Mark talks I look at my paint-stained hands that are now in small fists. It's a miracle I was able to keep them relaxed while we were at the border. Pam and Mark prepared me well. I am glad to be alive even though I'm scared about what I will find in the United States. I find it difficult to get a full breath. My heart aches when I think about my parents and brothers.

I have been Natalie Poland Ritchie for seventeen years. I have a good life here in the United States with my husband, Elliot, and my daughter, Gina. Only Elliot knows my story and my Iranian name. I have not had any contact with my family since I left Iran.

The doorbell rings and I assume it's my friend, Lucy, who's come to bake Christmas cookies like we've done for the past ten years. Now that our girls are older, they help us, and we have a great time. I call to her to come in as I turn up *Joy to the World*. I fling open the door. I stop dead in my tracks.

My mom and dad are standing on my front porch. I cry and then I laugh. My mom's eyes shine brightly. She holds out her arms and I walk into them. My dad surrounds us in a big bear hug. I shake and sob as we all move into the house. My daughter looks amazed as I speak Farsi to my parents. She looks exactly like her grandfather.

Joy to the World ends and Natalie Merchant begins to sing *It Came Upon a Midnight Clear*. When Elliot comes home, I will tell my daughter about the piercing of the veil. It is time, finally, to be free.

The Wavering

Five years ago Lucy was a mess after she and her husband, Bruce, had another fight. Lucy was angry. She didn't realize how angry she was until she was getting ready to go to her monthly book club who were meeting at Aspirus, the local bookstore and coffee shop. She prepared dinner for Bruce and the girls, but didn't eat with them because the group was having dinner at Aspirus followed by an author's talk on *Sugar Daddies*. Bruce didn't know that Bev had recently left her husband and was now living alone. Lucy didn't tell him this because she knew he would not like that Bev separated from her husband. But Bruce found out and he and Lucy had the fight that Lucy had wanted to avoid.

Lucy screamed at Bruce. "Who the fuck cares where Bev lives? The book club is the book club. That's it. I've been with this group of six women for years, Bruce. They're my friends. Things happen. People change, Bruce."

Lucy saw fear on her girl's faces. Georgia was eight. Sylvie was five. She kissed and hugged them goodbye and told them she loved them. She walked out the door without slamming it. That was the best she could do. What she didn't say was, *This group is my sanity. It's my monthly check-in. It's more than a book club. I have an unwavering friendship and trust with these women. We help each other get through good and bad times. Right now we're helping Bev get through a difficult separation with her husband.*

When Lucy returned that night, Bruce told her, "I'm taking the girls to my parents' house for the week. Think about what you want. You need to make some decisions, Lucy. I don't like a depressed, angry, unhappy wife."

The next morning before the car even left the driveway Lucy began crying. She wandered around the house aimlessly and ended up lying in bed that entire first day. She felt threatened and scared. Her whole world was falling apart. After that first day Lucy began to notice what she was feeling. She was unhappy. She was lost. She didn't know what to do with herself. She had too much free time, and no life outside her husband and daughters. Her girls were in school full-time now and she had to find new routines. Lucy was sick of Bruce bossing her around. She was tired of Bruce making all the decisions about their vacations and social events. He had even started telling her what clothes to wear. Recently he told her he did not want her to cut wood anymore.

Lucy missed cutting wood with her dad. During her childhood summers she and her dad cut wood together in preparation for the long winter. Bruce insisted she only stack it. To avoid a fight, she agreed.

When her husband and children returned, Lucy and Bruce talked. Lucy told him she wanted to go back to school and take classes. He was supportive as long as she only took day classes. At first she talked with him about her writing classes and read him her stories. He had a hard time listening, so she stopped reading her writing to him. Eventually she stopped telling him she was taking classes. He did not ask her anything about what she was doing.

Recently, Lucy talked to Bruce about his need to control her. She can't remember exactly what she said, but he told her what he expected of her in no uncertain terms. She stood quietly as he spoke to her. She walked out of the room when he stopped talking.

Later that night he informed her, "I'm taking the girls to my parents' house for a week and you better get herself together, Lucy. Get your priorities straight."

So here she is. Bruce and the girls are gone again. This time, though, Lucy is excited. It's been five long years since she's had a week to herself. She does not know exactly what she will do and she doesn't need to know. She trusts that her path will be revealed moment to moment.

After the three of them leave, Lucy calmly stands at the kitchen window washing the breakfast dishes. She sees Mr. Brown and his old Clydesdale, Bernice. Mr. Brown is wearing his familiar red cap and ratty green jacket. She knows he's going into the forest to cut wood. He's had a business selling firewood since Lucy was a child. Seeing him gives her comfort.

Mr. Brown has already delivered four cords of wood to Bruce and Lucy. It comes neat and tidy, the perfect length for the wood stove. At times Lucy misses cutting wood, but her life is busy now, so only having to stack it in the garage, is a relief. Her girls help her do that, now that they're older. Yesterday when the wheelbarrow tipped over, because the girls loaded it too full, they all laughed, and Lucy used that as a teaching moment about how to stack wood so it doesn't fall.

As she washes the dishes Lucy realizes she is uneasy. She is wavering, stay in her marriage, leave her marriage. So much is unspoken. Bruce has no idea Lucy is one class away from getting her BA in English. He has no idea she is writing a book. He doesn't know what she does all day. What he cares about is that she looks good, has sex with him whenever he wants, has dinner on the table when he gets home from work, keeps the house clean, and that his girls are well dressed, well behaved, and good students. He likes his world unwavering, the same routine every day.

This semester Lucy is taking an advanced creative writing class. She is flourishing. Professor Madeline Allen asked her to be her teaching assistant for two classes. The day class is no issue, but the night class poses a problem because Bruce continues to require that Lucy be home every night.

During her week alone, Lucy has time and space to think. She works long hours on her book, spends time with friends, and shares meals with some of her classmates. She decides she wants to separate from Bruce. She cannot stand his unwavering anymore, his need for everything to be in a certain order, his order, with no input from her. Lucy is tired of letting Bruce control her. She is sick of sneaking around behind his back because she's afraid to say what she wants, thinks, and believes. She is tired of her throat closing down when she wants to express herself. She does not like being afraid to speak. She can no longer tolerate her own silence.

During the week that Bruce and her girls are away, Lucy accepts the teaching assistant position and attends her first monthly afternoon gathering of Professor Allen's teaching assistants. She meets Cecilia at that gathering. Lucy is amazed how easy it is to talk to her. They have lunch together and set up a swim work-out date. She hopes that she and Cecilia can become friends.

This time when Bruce and the girls return, Lucy and Bruce do not talk. They resume their daily sex routine and attend a flurry of Bruce's holiday work parties. Lucy is her stunning, fit, well-dressed, self. She is careful not to drink too much like some of Bruce's colleagues' wives. Everything appears normal on the outside. At the dinner table the girls talk excitedly about hiking with Cecilia and her daughter, Cara. Surprisingly, Bruce has not grilled Lucy or the girls about Cecilia or Cara. He seems genuinely happy that his girls are in good spirits and that Georgia is losing her baby fat. He does not like overweight females. Lucy tells him she is working out at the pool, swimming laps.

One day after doing laps, Lucy starts crying in the shower. Cecilia sits outside the shower while Lucy sits on the tile-shower-floor sobbing and talks about feeling like she's starving. Afterwards they go to Aspirus and talk. Lucy no longer feels capable of carrying on with her life in spite of what she thinks and feels. Her friendship with Cecilia provides her with the support she needs to express her feelings. She knows what she needs to do. Lucy stops wavering.

She tells Bruce, "I'll be gone on Tuesday nights. I've accepted the teaching assistant position with Professor Allen."

Bruce stares at her. If looks could kill, Lucy would be dead.

The next morning, he informs her, "You will not take that job. You need to be home with your family in the evenings. You will tell Professor Allen you are sorry, but your family needs you."

What Bruce doesn't count on is that Lucy is no longer wavering. That second time her husband took her daughters to his parents, Lucy learned that nothing is certain. Everything changes. Do you accept the changing tide and take the risk? Or do you stay stuck? Lucy has accepted that her girls are growing up. They are ten and thirteen. Lucy wants to accept that she has a right to be happy.

After Bruce leaves for work, Lucy pulls out her suitcase and takes her clothes out of the dresser. She cannot stay here any longer. She carries her clothes to the car and loads her books into the empty blue plastic bins in the garage. She takes her toothbrush and leaves the toothpaste. When she thinks she's done, she goes back into the bedroom and gets her jewelry. She drives to a motel near the university and pays for a week while she looks for a place to live for her and her girls.

It isn't easy at first. Just like Bev's husband, Bruce hires an expensive lawyer and tries to get Lucy's parental rights revoked. It doesn't work. The girls stay with Bruce at first because he stays in the family home. In two months, Lucy has joint custody and her girls live with her half-time in a two-bedroom cottage within walking distance of the university. The girls accept that they have to share a bedroom until Sylvie goes to an out-of-state college.

Out of the wavering Lucy creates a new life. She works full time at the university and has recently been accepted into a PhD program. When Sylvie leaves for college, Georgia moves in full time with Lucy. Cecilia and Lucy are friends and colleagues. They have lunch together almost every day and on some of these days Cecilia's partner, Lola, joins them. They swim laps in the pool and challenge each other to swim a mile in less time. Bruce remarries and has two more daughters.

Lucy has shown her girls how to live with uncertainty. She has taught them how to sit with the discomfort of wavering and wait until clarity comes. When the clarity comes, she reminds them about the importance of being able to deal with change responsibly and take right action.

Lucy loves her creative life. It is an ongoing work-in-progress.

Mud Flats

My mother tells me, "Don't go into the mud-flats!"

"But I want to get to the river," I say in a whiny voice.

"There are other ways to get to the river, Cecilia."

When she doesn't call me Cece or Cees I know she's making a point, and I'm supposed to take her seriously. I listen. I heed her warnings until I'm a senior in high school.

Then I watch Jason go through the mud to get to the river. He dives in and stays in for a long time. The other kids leave before Jason returns to shore. I wait. When he gets out, he raises his arms and turns his eyes towards the sky. I see something in his face or think I do. He's far away. Could I have even seen his face? Probably not. It's his body language that holds his triumph.

You might expect conquering from a teenage boy, like he completes a task or does a rite of passage and is now part of some club. But it isn't like that for Jason. His triumph is a spiritual change, a deep rearranging of his psyche. At seventeen we don't talk about the rearranging of the psyche. We don't have that language. I ask him lots of questions. He gives every one of my questions consideration and tries to answer them.

He tells me, "When I dove in, the water was clear underneath, Cees. Only the top layer was black."

I am mesmerized by his words. I tell him, "I want to slog through the mud-flats, too, and go in the Black Thrush River."

Jason nods and says, "Let me know when you're ready. I'll wait for you at the edge of the flats, right where you waited for me. It's important to go alone. It's a singular journey, an initiation of sorts. It changes you, Cees. That's what I know."

And I want to be changed. My yearning to go through the muck and end up at the river is stronger since Jason did it. I'm tired of being Cecilia Ryder, the smart girl who is college-bound, who follows mommy and daddy's rules, the good girl. It takes me three months to get up enough courage.

On a quiet Thursday afternoon in May I say good-bye to Jason and begin walking across the mud-flats. Jason is the only one there. I don't want anyone else. Some kids, boys mostly, make a big spectacle of the whole thing. I don't want any fanfare. No girls in my class had done it, or none that I know.

The mud is hard at first and I can walk easily. Then the mud becomes wet and one of my boots gets stuck. I sit down and pull my foot out. Jason didn't tell me about the mud swallowing up his boots. I don't know if that happened to him or not, but I know I want to be careful because I don't like getting stuck. I keep my eyes on the ground and find ground that is less wet. I pay attention and focus. At the same time, I keep moving towards the river. The river and the aspens are always in my sight.

I take off my boots and walk in my bare feet. I feel the wind on my arms and face. I see an Indian woman and her small child. I want to call out to her, but I don't. When I get to where I saw her, she's not there. What is there is a small, deep, clear pool of water and a clay water vessel. I stop and get a drink. I feel the water circulating throughout my body. I feel like I'm being cleansed.

When I get to the river I walk into the cool black water and dive deep. The water is surprisingly blue underneath the blackness. I do not want to resurface, but of course I do. I have to breathe. I continue deep diving and each time I am able to stay underneath the water longer. I get the feeling that I'm supposed to find something. The fifth and final time I submerge myself, I see a small statue. It looks like a woman but I can't really tell what it is. I pull on it, and after three strong pulls, she's free. I come back to the surface and breathe deeply.

When I look at the object I see a woman with a water vessel in the crook of her arm. She's a water-carrier. I love her from the moment I see her. I have no idea why I start crying.

I must have been in the Black Thrush River for a long time because the sun is going down and I hear birds chirping. I need to make my way back across the flats before dark. I put the water-carrier in my boots and sling them over my shoulder. I see the Indian woman again. This time she's holding her child's hand and they're walking towards the river. I smile.

When I get back to the edge of the flats Jason is there. We look at each other and he holds me as I cry. We do not exchange a single word and I never tell him about the water-carrier. I have no need or desire to talk about my experience. He is my witness. For this, I am grateful.

We graduate from high school a week later. Jason leaves town to work at a dude ranch in Arizona and I waitress at a local restaurant. I swim in the Black Thrush after work nearly every day that summer. I enter the river at the old Conley bridge where the water has been dammed and there is a swimming hole. I do not walk the mudflats again.

In the spring of my first year at college, I cross paths with Lola, who also grew up in Morrison. We graduated from Four Corners High School but we weren't friends. She ran with the rough crowd, the drinkers and the druggies, the bad boys and girls. But both Lola and I ended up at Vassar. Apparently, she is smart too.

I don't recognize her at first. She isn't in her usual black. Her dyed black hair is now blonde. And although she isn't preppy, she isn't goth anymore either. She's toned down. I'm different too. We come from opposite directions and now both of us are more in the middle, although we both miss living on the edge. We like pushing the limits, not quite fitting in, not really wanting to. We both have a higher calling.

The mud-flats come up in our conversation.

Lola tells me, "I watched you cross the mud-flats."

I find this hard to believe.

"I didn't see you there."

"No, I watched you from the edge by the concrete post."

I know the place. Only if you grew up in Morrison would you know that place.

"I watched Jason watching you. I envied you. I went in a week after you, but I was alone. I had no one to witness me doing it. I saw how it changed you."

I look at her, surprised. "But you didn't know me."

"I didn't have to. I saw the change. It was all over you. You had a glow, a fire burning deep within. I saw it in Jason, too, but I related more to you, another girl. It changed me too," she said quietly, matter-of-factly.

Lola and I begin to get together regularly at college and eventually we become lovers. Twenty years later, we are still lovers.

Every spring we return to Morrison and walk the mud-flats to the river. We carry the sculpture of the water-carrier with us and immerse her in the water. When it's warm enough we dive into the Black Thrush together, going deep below the surface, frolicking like maidens. We hope the baby girl that Lola is carrying will love these flats and the river as much as we do.

We are the lucky ones. We did not get stuck in Morrison, but we do appreciate how the journey through the mud-flats to the river changed our lives. And although our daughter, Cara, will not grow up in Morrison, we will expose her to the power of the mud-flats and the Black Thrush River. We will let the water work its magic.

Unravelling

In the middle of the night I get a call from my Aunt Polly.

"Your dad died about an hour ago. Your mother found him dead in bed. She's not doing well. I'm so sorry, Lynda."

I tell my aunt, "I'll come as soon as I can. I want to fly out of Palm Springs, it's easier than driving to Los Angeles. I'll let you know when my flight will get there." Short and to the point. That's how my aunt and I have always communicated. It works.

I am robotic. I get my flight and begin packing. I'm having difficulty reconciling the healthy man I saw two summers ago with my dead dad. I am as quiet as I can be, but my partner, Alise, wakes up when I'm packing.

Alise is angry. But that's nothing new. We've been fighting most of the past two years. I have no idea how things got this bad, and right now I don't care. My dad is dead and I have to catch a cross-country flight.

"What are you doing?"

"I'm packing. My dad died a few hours ago. I'm leaving in three hours."

Alise stares at me. I look away and begin rummaging around in my drawers. I'm trying to find the right clothes to take. I hear only the end of something Alise is saying.

"…a pattern." She spats at me.

I do not respond. I'm weary. I do not want to fight.

Alise raises her voice and talks at me through pursed lips, "Are you listening to me Lynda? I'm talking to you. I'm so sick of you not telling me what you're feeling. It's a bad pattern of yours."

I don't hear anything Alise says before, *a bad pattern.* But it doesn't really matter because we've been having this same fight for the past two years. I don't even listen to her anymore. I can repeat the entire conversation, like it's a script in a play. Lately I've begun thinking about *Who's Afraid of Virginia Woolf* when Alise starts her rant. It's my new way of shutting her off. This time I'm back in my childhood, sledding with my dad, throwing snowballs, and being happy drinking hot cocoa with marshmallows. We had so much fun. My mother never participated in these activities and was always resentful that her husband and daughter were having fun together.

I finish packing. I'm aware the room is silent. I glance at Alise. She's staring at me.

"When are you coming back?"

"I don't know."

Alise pushes. "A week, a month?"

I look at her then. What I think is, *You haven't even said you're sorry about my dad dying. Why are you pushing me?* I'm angry and hurt. I breathe. I hear the honking cab.

I say, "I'm not coming back."

I didn't plan on saying this. I don't really know if it's what I want. And even when it comes out of my mouth, I don't know if it's true. Alise is surprisingly silent. We stare at each other. I turn and walk out of our bedroom. We don't say good-bye.

When I arrive at my childhood home I become my mother's caretaker. I learn she has cancer, that she is dying. I make arrangements with Ellen Baylor, the hospice nurse. She sets up twenty-four-hour-a-day-care for my mother. Every morning I sit by my mother's bed and read her stories, pay her bills, and write her correspondence. We laugh and cry and talk.

Yesterday my mother told me, "I love you, Lynda. Thank you for taking care of me."

I hold her hand and we cry together until Aunt Polly walks in. Then my mom and her sister tell stories about their childhood, some of which I have not heard. The three of us laugh and cry together. Peace, love, and acceptance permeate the room. I end that night reading my mother a couple of chapters of *Jane Eyre* until she falls asleep.

The next day, four months to the day my dad died, Ellen stops me outside my mom's door and says softly, "She's slipped into a coma, probably has hours to a few days left." Ellen squeezes my shoulder gently.

I shudder and ask her to call my Aunt Polly. I walk into Mom's room where she is resting peacefully. I think, *Dying is so weird. Last night mom was smiling and laughing. Now she's lying in a coma.* I sit and look at her. Then I pick up her hand and hold it. I begin reading *Jane Eyre*. We are close to the book's end. When I finish the book, I hear my mom's breathing change. She squeezes my hand, although this seems so unlikely that I wonder if it really happened. Then there is silence.

I do not immediately call Ellen. I don't know how long I sit in the room holding my dead mother's hand. I feel immense gratitude that I was able to take care of my mom the last four months of her life. We were not close when I was a child, but in these last four months my mom and I formed a bond.

After the funeral I do not know what I'm going to do. I spend the mornings by myself. In the afternoon I go to Aspirus where I sit and read by the fire, talk to the locals, and join a book group that meets once a month and a writing group that comes together weekly. I walk in the woods nearly every day. Aunt Polly and I have dinner together most nights.

A week after my mother's funeral I call Alise and tell her my mom died.

There is a slight exhale of air and a cursory, "Lynda, I'm sorry," followed by silence. After more silence, Alise asks, "Are you coming back?" Not home, but back.

"I don't think so." Neither of us speaks again. Alise hangs up.

I call Rena and ask if she'll pack up my studio. Rena says yes. I give her a brief version of my last contact with Alise. Rena knows about our conversation from a friend who's now seeing Alise.

"It's over, so much loss," I murmur. "Hard to bear."

"Yes," Rena says softly. "Do you want me to send you anything?"

Rena ships my clothes, books, jewelry, art, writings, and journals, everything in my studio except the furniture. Rena and I talk on the phone once a week.

As I stand at the large picture window looking out at the snow-covered pines and hemlocks, I watch snow flurries dance. I've loved this view since she I was a little girl. Spring is in the air even though it's cold.

It's been nine months since my life unraveled. I've picked up the pieces and am creating a new life here. While I stand at the large picture window I see a small figure in the distance. As the person gets closer, I recognize Rena, rosy-cheeked, wearing a purple Peruvian wool hat, red down jacket, and L.L. Bean boots. She waves. I smile. Rena is here, hopefully to stay.

The Book Signing

In the early evening, the woman walks into Aspirus. She's been looking for a place to sit that isn't large and busy. She tried sitting at the library, but it was too quiet. She needed more action. She wanted a place filled with books, a place where she can feel people's energy and hear quiet conversation and occasional blurts of laughter or anger. She sees a sign saying Book Reading tonight. There's a mousy looking woman standing by a small table. She has medium length brown hair pulled back with a black pearl clasp and is wearing a straight black skirt and chunky shoes. Her name tag pinned on her light blue Peter-Pan collar says Adriana.

The woman goes to the table and asks Adriana, "What's the book that's going to be discussed?"

Adriana looks her directly in the eye, and the woman is struck by the piercing blue eyes which are mostly hidden behind large, round, black, professorial-like glasses. Adriana's gaze doesn't waver. That surprises the woman.

"*Sugar Daddies*," Adriana says.

"*Sugar Daddies*?" The woman says.

"That's right."

The woman wants to say, *What kind of a book is that? What's it about?* But she doesn't. She returns her gaze to Adriana who hands her a half-page typed description of the book. The woman skims this while she continues standing directly in front of her. Adriana's eyes never leave the woman's face. When the woman looks up, she smiles, and Adriana smiles back.

"Have you read it?" the woman asks.

Adriana nods with a glint in her eye, something that seems to beg the woman to say more. But the woman doesn't say more, and there is silence. The woman begins to feel a little tipsy.

Adriana says through the woman's fogginess, "Ma'am, are you alright?"

She asks this question twice before the woman responds.

"Yes, yes. I must be a bit hungry. I'm feeling a bit shaky. Need to eat something." Her voice trails off.

Adriana wants to touch the woman's arm and support her, but she doesn't allow herself this kind of intimacy. Adriana cannot afford to do that right now. She knows herself well enough to know that if she crosses that boundary, she will not be able to give the talk about her book, *Sugar Daddies*. She will not be able to paint a picture of the strange, dark, dangerous underworld where she lived for a year, a place most people do not know exists and if they do know it exists, they do not want to acknowledge it.

Adriana looks at the woman. The woman looks back.

When the woman finally speaks, she says, "I'll just get a cup of tea and a biscuit. What time does the reading start?"

"Eight o'clock," answers Adriana.

The woman looks at her watch and says mostly to herself or so it seems to Adriana. "Hmm. Seven now. Okay."

She turns and walks towards the small cafe. The woman does not look at Adriana again. Adriana's blue eyes follow her. As she watches the woman glide slowly down the aisle, Adriana feels her stomach clench. She knows this woman.

Adriana is not the only one in disguise.

The Mouse In The Guard House

I can't believe I get to Aspirus before it opens. I'm not sure what I'm looking for, but something gets me out of the house earlier than usual. I talk briefly to the owner, Zoe, then head to the non-fiction section.

I'm looking at titles and thumbing through books when I hear a woman say, *The Mouse in the Guard House.* I stop dead in my tracks and go right back to when Jason gave me that book.

I was up early stretching, Peets Coffee brewing in the kitchen. I heard the hummingbird wings beat as the birds drank the sweet red nectar outside my kitchen window. The intercom to the gate buzzed. Nobody had the audacity to come to my house in the morning. Everyone who mattered to me knew morning was my writing time, my time to be alone. I did not like to be disturbed. I thought about not answering the call, but the intercom continued to buzz.

Charlotte, I need to see you, called Jason. I buzzed open the gate.

I flung open the door and pretended to be put out, but I wasn't. Jason wasn't the kind of guy who interrupted people without good reason. *Yes,* I said with my hands on my hips.

Jason stood there with his hands stretched out holding a package wrapped in blue paper with the world on it and a red bow on top. I looked at him with a raised eyebrow. I could see he was excited.

He bowed and said, Merry Christmas, Charlotte.
For moi? I curtsied.

I learned later he found *The Mouse in the Guard House* in his grandmother's attic. It had fallen behind some other books when he was going through her stuff. He told me that she read it to him when he was young, but it wasn't really a children's book. He was sure I would love the story.

By this time I started to feel impatient. I had begun my morning ritual where I sit with coffee in hand and put pen to paper. I felt interrupted because I was interrupted. Jason wanted to tell me about the book and his grandmother. I only heard a few words before

I shut him down. I thanked him for the book. At least I did that. He asked me to read it, and I was noncommittal. What a bitch I can be!

I got caught up in my life, and when he called a week later I realized I hadn't even opened the package. I've got to hand it to him. He was patient and persistent. Eventually I opened the package. It wasn't a long book, about a hundred pages. It had a green hard cover with large blocky black letters that said, *The Mouse in the Guard House* by Houston Wings. When I saw the title, I wasn't interested in the book.

Jason kept checking in weekly. Six weeks went by before he finally said, *Okay Charlotte, it looks like you're not going to read it.*

His statement jolted me.

I stop reminiscing and tune back into the two women talking in the next aisle.

"The book changed my life. There's this mouse who really isn't a mouse at all. It's a symbol for the part of Carolyn that is small and scared. She lives in a guard house on just the other side of a tall wrought-iron fence with a locked gate. She buzzes in guests who come to visit Mr. and Mrs. Wiggins. Since both the Wiggins died, the big house is in ruins. The stones around the entryway have crumbled, and the old oak door hangs on one hinge. Carolyn continues to live in her tiny house. Now she doesn't have to let anyone onto the property unless she wants to."

The woman is breathless as she speaks to her friend who has not yet uttered a single word. I am dumb-struck. This is the story Jason wanted me to read? Her brief description makes me aware that the author may have captured my life story.

"How did it change your life?" The woman asks.

"Well, you know how scared and unsure I've been about what to do..."

I strain to hear her, but she's lowered her voice so I cannot hear her last words.

I never read the book, and Jason eventually stopped asking. Then he drifted away. I don't know where he is now. Like most friendships I have, I don't put much energy into them. I forget I like people.

"Oh, I'm so happy for you."

Again I'm pulled back into the moment with the friend's words.

———

149

I nod to Zoe on my way out and begin running down the street to my car. I need to get to my house behind a chain-link fence with a locked gate. I want to find the book and read it. Then I will find Jason.

Holy

I don't know your name at first. I see you at Asprius. We are not friends. I call you Holy because you wear that sweater with the three neat holes. The holes in my sweater never look neat. They're always running, threads askew, and their unravelling is imminent. It drives my crazy mother crazier. She can't stand the unravelling and my messy look, but I don't care what she thinks and feels about this.

I refer to you as Holy one day to Zoe, who looks at me with surprise.

"You like her Carson, don't you?"

I hadn't thought of this. I hadn't needed to. But I do notice when Zoe says it, I feel a tiny stirring, a bit of an opening that eventually becomes a crack, and then I can't hold back the dam. But I'm getting ahead of myself here.

That day I just feel a little tingle or twinge, some slight tightening or is it a loosening, around my heart. I felt discomfort. That's what I know today. Was I so out of touch back then that I couldn't even name the feeling? Probably. I could not identify my feelings for a long time. I didn't remember people's names. Sometimes I was surprised I remembered Zoe's name, but she'd been around for a lot of years and had endeared herself to me early on, before the big close down where nothing and no one got in. But that's a story I'm not interested in telling right now and maybe not ever.

It's you, Holy, that I want to talk about, you with your sweater with the three neat holes that I eventually learn have that silky tape underneath them to keep the holes from spreading. When I finally talk to you, you hold your own. You look at me and aren't particularly interested in answering any of my questions, but you do listen. When I begin to talk about the holes in my sweater, I see a shift in your face. It's slight, but it isn't a nothing. It's a something. I don't know what it means, but I want to find out. I go into great detail about my favorite grey and green wool sweater that's a wreck.

"I'd like to see it," you say.

I'm surprised.

"Okay," I say reluctantly, and your face changes from simpy grin to surprise and then something else, like irritation maybe.

151

"I'd like to see it," you repeat.

I think, *why?*

You say, "I like sweaters with holes."

You state the obvious, go right to the point. You seem sincere.

"Why?" I ask out loud this time.

"I don't know. I like holes in sweaters."

"What does that mean?" I ask.

"You don't get that?" Your voice rises a bit, and there's an edginess in your tone. "What part don't you get? My liking holes? My liking sweaters? My liking of holes in sweaters?"

And then, there is silence. We stare at each other. Your big blue eyes shine brightly. I know I am not getting any more information today. There is something angry and defiant about your response, and also a sadness.

I say, "Okay. I'll bring it."

I want to ask you about your anger and sadness, but I don't. I practice restraint, which is something I have never been good at.

I wear the sweater two weeks later when I meet you at Aspirus for a book signing. My mother would not like me appearing in public in this old ratty sweater, but you love it.

You fondle the threads and say, "What a beautiful sweater!"

And it is. It's old and has character.

As we talk that day at length about sweaters, I get it! For you, the holes in the sweater bring out the personality strengths of its owner, and this is what you love. And you love that I call you Holy, not H-O-L-E-Y, but H-O-L-Y. I don't learn your name, Charlotte Fitzpatrick, until you hire me to trim your ficus trees. I don't need to. You are always Holy to me.

The Chain-Link Fence

After you and I buy the land on the outskirts of town, Ethan, the first thing we do is put up the chain-link fence to insure that our property is clearly defined. Clear boundaries make it more difficult for people to wander in. Neither of us want a random visitor.

After the house is built, people have to buzz the intercom to get to the house. I get to make a decision whether I answer the call. From the street you cannot tell if anyone is home. I like it this way.

We bought the property because of the lake. I have mostly let go of the *we* now. You've been gone a long time, Ethan. The ficus were only mid-way up the fence. Now they are taller than the fence. They have softened the grey metal. I like that the chain-link fence is barely visible now. The two lines of trees we planted, one inside the fence and the other outside, give a double layer of protection and beauty. I could say barrier, yet it doesn't feel like a barrier to me.

Carson, the gardener, comes once a month to trim the double layer of ficus. I don't want them impeding my view of the lake. I took him some lemonade the other day and we ended up sitting on the back patio that overlooks the lake. Carson and I talked for several hours about the property and how it's changed since we bought it. Carson told me that he's lived in this village all his life and has seen a lot of changes. I felt comfortable talking with him, Ethan.

After he left I began thinking about how I became a young widow. I never wanted to be a widow, Ethan. We had been married seven years, and you had made a bundle of money. You were a wheeler and a dealer. With me you were just Ethan, not Ethan Livingston, like your mother called you, and not Ethan Livingston Fitzpatrick, the accomplished entrepreneur, just Ethan, smart, funny, social, sexy.

Some of my friends saw you as perfect, but you weren't. Your parents never understood why you married me, why we built this house on the lake, and why we put up a chain-link fence before we built the house.

I like the fence. I got it right early on. I needed the freedom to be able to choose when I have contact with people. If I don't have that freedom of choice, I am gnarly, which means I'm picky, difficult to get along with, and not all that nice. I can easily run a conversation amuck. Not a pretty scene.

You used to say, *In and out, Charlotte*, short for, *whoever you want in, is in, and the others need to stay out.* People didn't know you were that clear, Ethan. They thought I was the only one who wanted to limit visitors to our home. But you didn't want your parents to drop by and at first they felt they could. You nipped that in the bud quickly. Of course, they thought it was me. I heard your mother discussing it with you after she couldn't get in and had to call you from a pay phone in town. She was livid. She blamed me for your isolation and the fence. She never accepted this about you, even though you told her in no uncertain terms, *I wanted the fence, mother. It was all my idea. I am the driver of this train.* She never believed you.

At a pre-Christmas dinner, she turned to me and made a comment about the fence. You repeated what you had told her before. You stood up and said, *I want the fence, Mother. I determine who comes in. No one comes in unless I want them to. That's it. Charlotte has nothing to do with the fence. If you accuse her again, I will never invite you to our house.*

I must say it was a dramatic moment. There was a long silence. Then your father bucked up and said, *you can't talk to your mother that way, son.* You turned to him and put your hand out like a stop sign. Your mother was furious, but she got the message. She wasn't a stupid woman. The lines were drawn. She definitely understood that you would ban her, and she didn't want that.

We saw very little of them during the seven years of our marriage. Seven years, Ethan. I loved you so much, and you loved me. And then I flew alone to Paris. I called your parents about your accident after I identified your body. They wanted to come to Paris, but I told them I was bringing you back to the United States and would bury you in our small village cemetery. Your mother wanted you in the family plot, but your will was clear. You wanted the trees, the lake view, the history, and the quiet. Your parents cut me off after the funeral. There was no reason for us to continue having a relationship.

As I sit on the porch talking with Carson, I realize I'm ready to move on. He's the first man I've been interested in since you died.

We might be able to make a go of it. You would like him, Ethan. He's a lot like you. He likes the fence and the ficus.

Agnes

At The Casino

I see her that night at The Casino. She looks different from most of the people who come here. She's fit, tan, healthy-looking, and appears to be drinking water. She's laughing. No cigarette is hanging out of her mouth. No guys are clustered around her like dogs in heat. It looks like she's alone.

Butch comes up and pokes me.

"Smitten?" He asks.

I laugh. He nods. He's taking over my blackjack table while I go on my dinner break. When I laugh she looks over at me, and we stare at each other. I wonder who's going to drop their gaze first. It ends up being me. She's bold. I file this as I head toward her, keeping my eyes on her. She's smiling and still looking at me. Direct eye contact. What am I going to say? I'm not usually that assertive with women.

I make my way across the floor and say, "Hi. I'm Darren. I'm on my break now. Do you want to join me for dinner? I've got an hour and a half, then I'm back at the table for four more hours."

"Well Darren. I'm Cate. I'd love to have dinner with you, well, sit with you. I'm not hungry, so I'll just tag along."

I tell her, "I don't usually spend my dinner hour with people. I go to BeeBee's Diner, where you can get good cheap food and quiet. I usually read."

Cate says, "I've seen the sign, but I've never gone in."

"They've got good food, and I love Agnes. She's the waitress who's there most nights. She makes sure I get the little table in the southeast corner so I can have some privacy, which is a relief after the noise and lights of The Casino."

We walk the rest of the way in silence. When we walk into BeeBee's, Agnes greets me with a big smile and a hug.

"And who's this?" she asks as she looks at Cate.

"I'm Cate."

"Welcome," she says, never taking her eyes off Cate. Then she turns to me and says, "Your table's ready, Darren. Do you want the special?"

I nod.

"Would you like to see a menu?" she asks Cate.

"No. I'll just have a cup of jasmine tea with lemon, extra hot, please." Cate smiles at Agnes.

At dinner Cate and I talk about the books we're reading. That's it mostly. I call it our first date. Cate calls it The Encounter. What can I say? Butch was right. I was smitten. Cate was tired of fast-talking guys with a lot of superficial, empty words filling blank space, men who wanted to get her into bed. It's not that I didn't want to sleep with her, I did. There was something about her that I couldn't get enough of. After all these years together, I still can't get enough of her. She's not like any woman I've ever met. Cate The Invincible. Cate, the heroine of all my stories. You may be thinking I've idealized her, and I probably have, but I don't care.

That night I hugged Agnes goodbye and Agnes hugged both of us. Cate put her arm through mine and we walked arm in arm from BeeBee's Diner back to The Casino. I asked if I could see her after work.

"What time?" she asked.

"I'm done at 2 a.m."

"I'll be long asleep." I looked surprised. "I'm a day girl."

"But you came to The Casino tonight. Why?" I ask.

"I heard The Voice say, *Go to The Casino. Something's happening at The Casino.*"

"The Voice?" I ask quizzically.

She's quiet. We reach the employee's orange door.

"So, you'll be asleep?" I look at her and she looks back. I take a breath, "So... can I come sleep with you?"

She smiles. "Sleep?"

"Yes," I say. "I'm actually a day guy too, but I took this job at The Casino because I needed a job and it pays good." I take out my key card.

She does the sexy, direct-eye-contact-thing and says, "My address is 2714 Brighton, Apartment C. Go through the gate on the left-hand side of the big house. It's not locked. I'm the only one back there. A and B are in the front. Mine's the little cottage, green with orange trim, a fifteen-minute walk from here. I'll leave the door unlocked and the light on in the living room. Lock it after you come in."

I look at her with a huge grin and repeat, "2714 Brighton, off Camry?"

"Yup," she says. "Small street. Five houses. You can't miss it." She squeezes my right forearm and is gone.

I can't stop thinking about Cate my entire shift. I find her house after work and we actually do sleep. When she leaves early in the morning for work, she tells me to lock up when I leave. I write her a note asking if she wants to meet me at BeeBee's that night.

Cate meets me at BeeBee's and we have dinner together. I tell her about Agnes, "She's been like a mother to me ever since I got to Savannah. Her son was killed by a grenade in Viet Nam when he was twenty-one, my age now. She needed a son and I needed a mother."

When Cate and I are leaving, Agnes hugs me and whispers, "This one's a keeper, Darren. I'm happy for you."

She hugs Cate, too.

That night after work I go to Cate's again. When we wake up, we talk all morning because neither one of us has to go to work. I tell her that I left my parent's house when I was sixteen after witnessing another fight where my father hit my mother. I called the police that time. When they got to the house my mother and father blamed me for their problems. My mother was furious that the cops took my dad to jail. They were both drunk and I was sick of being caught in the middle. My parents wanted me to choose one over the other, but when I did, they got angry at me and teamed up against me. I left with a backpack stuffed with a couple changes of clothes. I've been alone ever since, a man without a past, at least not one I wanted to claim.

With Cate, my history catches up with me. Relationships can do that if they're worth anything. The first time Cate and I fought I got deadly calm, and when Cate did not cancel her meeting with a male friend, I screamed at her. She walked out on me. She didn't come home that night and I never went to sleep. I was frantic. I was acting just like my father, except I didn't hit her and I wasn't drunk.

"You're a slut," I shouted.

"No, Darren. I have a friend who I haven't seen in a long time and he and I are going to have dinner together. That's it."

"You should have told me he was coming to town."

"I am telling you. He called me half an hour ago."

"I don't believe you. You're lying."

"No, Darren. I am not lying. Why would you think that? I never lie to you."

"You told me this guy walked out on you and you hadn't had any contact with him in years."

"Yes. That's true. And now he's called and asked me to meet him. I want to meet with him. I hope to get some resolution."

"Isn't it already resolved? It's been five years, hasn't it? What's to resolve? And why dinner? Why not lunch?"

"What difference does it make, Darren? Lunch or dinner? What's the big deal?"

"You're having dinner at his hotel. It will be really easy to just pop on up to his room and sleep with him."

"Are you kidding?"

"Well. I know you liked sex with him. Hell! You like sex. You've had sex with a lot of men. That's what you do when you want to feel loved. You have indiscriminate sex with whoever crosses your path."

You left after my final nasty comment. I wanted to stop you, but I didn't. I called you and left messages. Then I texted you. You ignored me and I got scared that you were never coming home. I thought about going to the hotel restaurant where I knew you were meeting him, but I stopped myself. I was awake all night. I realized I was acting just like my drunken father.

When we finally talked I apologized and said I was sorry. You listened and suggested I get help. I told you I would, and I did.

In therapy we learned how to fight. We learned about our patterns, our triggers, and how to forgive one another. We clawed our way to grace. We say that to each other when we're fighting. It breaks the tension and reminds us to stop, take a breath, and listen to each other.

So there you have it. We're ten years into this relationship, and it seems like we're both in it for good. I'm still clawing my way to grace. It doesn't get better than that.

Neon Lights

The first time I saw a diner was in an old movie from the 50's. My dad and I were curled up on the couch. It was probably a Saturday night. I remember the flashing neon sign, Betty's Diner. I loved the bright pink lights blinking on and off. Pink has never been my favorite color, but still, I loved those pink lights.

My father told me, "You love the glitz, Erika."

And I did. And I do.

When I was six years old I did a tap performance. I was one of fifteen bees with girls of all shapes and sizes dressed in blue satin leotards with glistening black sequins. My grandmother made my costume. I had a blue headband with antennae decorated with the same shiny black sequins. I loved the silky feel of the satin and the way the sequins sparkled. I felt like a million bucks.

Somehow the movie with Betty's Diner and my bee dance performance were tied together. It wasn't until high school when I starred in the play, *Nora Goes to New York*, that I understood the connection. In the play I experienced another flashing neon light. This one flashed *NORA* in red neon. I danced my heart out those nights. I loved moving all around the stage doing leg-kick-ups. I dreamt of being a real Rockette. My father told me it was possible, and I believed him.

Quite early my dad had *The Secret* thing down.

"Build it and they will come." He said. "Have clear intentions and you will manifest your dreams."

That was the last thing my father said to me as he left for work that night. I'd only been asleep a couple of hours when I heard the pounding on our front door. I was irritated at first because I'd been woken out of a sound sleep. I saw the police cruisers blinking their red lights. I thought my dad might be playing some trick on me. He knew I loved flashing lights. So at first I decided to ignore the ruckus, but the policemen kept pounding on the door. I glanced at my clock. It read 3:13 a.m. Then I heard my name being called. I didn't know what was happening. When I opened the door I was kind of bitchy. I knew all the cops in town because my dad had been a cop for a long time. They let me off two times when they picked me up drunk. They brought me home. My dad told me after the second time, that the next time I got picked up, they would take me to Juvenile Hall. I didn't really believe him. I also didn't feel like pushing my luck. That's when my dad, Sandy, and I watched *The Secret* together. That was their first date. It was the first woman he'd gone out with since my mother left us seven years ago. I was used to it being just him and me. But I liked her, and I could see that he really liked her. I was happy for him, although I was a little jealous, too.

Roger and Seth were at the door. They came in and told me to sit down. I knew something was terribly wrong.

"What's going on?" My voice was loud, really loud. Roger guided me to a chair and Seth helped me sit.

"Where's Dad?" I barked.

"There's been an accident, Erika."

"Is he at the hospital?"

"Yes."

I stood up. "Let's go."

Roger said, "It's bad, Erika."

"I want to see him."

"The accident was bad."

"Let's go." I repeated.

When I got in the police car, Seth drove like a bat out of hell. My mind was going crazy. I knew my dad was still alive, but I didn't know what bad meant and I didn't ask. At the hospital they escorted me into the emergency room. I saw the doctors working on my mangled father. They let me go to him. I took his hand. I realized then what bad meant. He looked like death warmed over. I barely recognized his smashed in face. They had his body covered with a white blanket.

"Daddy?"

I felt a slight squeeze and I heard him whisper, "Love you, E."

And then the doctor told Roger to take me out. They had to do the surgery.

Roger and Seth sat with me and Sandy showed up. I sat there, stoic. A cop's daughter. My dad died on the table. Too many injuries. The rest is a blur.

So here I am sitting at another diner, BeeBee's. I was on my way to Savannah for a job interview when the rain started coming down like cats and dogs. The road was slick and I could barely see, just like the night my dad died in that car accident. I saw the lights blinking in the distance and knew I needed to pull over. When I walked in, a waitress with Agnes embroidered on her smock, came up to me and asked if I wanted coffee. I said yes.

That's how it began. Business was slow and Agnes and I got to talking. I ended up telling her about my dad and she talked about her son. We connected. When I got the job I came back to let her know I would be living in Savannah now. She was happy for me. I was happy I had someone to talk to who understood about death and loss.

Now that I'm living here I stop into BeeBee's most days after work. I sit at the counter and chat with Agnes. She's become a second mother to me and I am the daughter she always wished she had.

BeeBee's Diner

My mom was a normal mom until my father died unexpectedly. After that she had a lot of men coming in and out of her bedroom. They weren't necessarily nice men, but they paid well and that's how she supported us. At some point I became a distraction because I was young, had nice tits, and the men wanted me instead of her.

Jimmy put his hands on me one day, and I fought him off while my mother stood there watching with a look on her face I couldn't even begin to understand. I left. I was almost seventeen. I found women who want women. I like women, although in the end I still became my mother, without men and money being exchanged.

Truth: I wanted a different life.

Truth: I didn't know how to change.

Truth: I decided to move and I hoped it would work out.

You might wonder if it's that simple. I can tell you my *truths* got me packed and on the road. I heard a voice in my head commanding me to drive south. I surprised myself and listened. I must have been desperate because I don't usually respond well to being told what to do.

I'm finding my place in the south. I'm living poor because I don't want to go through my savings too quickly. Today I woke up sweaty and alone.

I'm lonely. I want sex. I've got a good body, not too thin and not too fat. I'd say I'm medium, just right. My body's been an asset, and it's gotten me into trouble, too. I have a tendency to gain weight if I'm not careful, so I carry a scale with me everywhere I go. I weigh myself every morning. My weight determines what I eat that day. Today I weigh in light, 133, so I decide I'll go to BeeBee's Diner with its large white sign with black blocky letters. The sign looks like it came right out of the Fifties. I'm hungry because I left that little hole of a room where I'm staying without having breakfast.

I've only been living here a short time, and I don't know anyone. I haven't found a job or a woman to have sex with. And this is my problem: Men like me, and all I want are women.

I walk into BeeBees on my way to Tybee Beach and find a home. Dan, the boss, thinks I'm there because of the sign in the window, *Waitress Wanted*. That isn't why I walk in, but he looks me over and must see something in me that I don't even know is there. He puts me to work serving coffee, making small talk, and getting acquainted with the locals. He tells me that his head waitress, Agnes, had a doctor's appointment today and that she'll be in tomorrow. He tells me she's a mainstay here and will show me the ropes. I find my niche.

Soon after I get the waitress job at BeeBee's I move into a small, run-down house that has a hot plate, a pint-size fridge, and insufficient air conditioning. It's only five miles away from the diner, down a dirt road, right on the Savannah River. Over time I've fixed it up nice.

I've been waiting tables at BeeBee's for two years. I love Agnes. She's the mother I never had. We work together four days a week. I've spent the big holidays with her and last year I took my girlfriend, who doesn't live with me, but I feel like we'll be living together soon. I'm starting school next week.

BeeBee's and Agnes and Dan saved my life.

Truth: When I look in the mirror, I don't see my mother anymore.

Truth: I'm happy most days.

Truth: I still weigh myself every day and get to eat biscuits one day a week.

Truth: If I can change my life, anyone can.

Hemingway wakes to the barking dog again and glances at her digital clock, 3:13 a.m. How many days has it been? Eleven? Fifteen? She'll have to look in her journal. She still hasn't decided if 3:13 a.m. is morning or the middle of the night. What she does know is that she wakes at precisely 3:13 a.m. and hears the barking dog. The barking has become her morning chimes, like the bells she used to wake to when she lived in that little village in the Andes mountains.

This 3:13 a.m., when Hemingway first hears the dog and its mournful bark, she struggles to come awake. She remembers her dream which is more like a nightmare. She's floating in a sea in a small blue dinghy with no paddles, watching her parents drown. When her parents stop flailing and their frantic sounds end, the turbulent water suddenly becomes still. Paddles appear. Hemingway rows over to where she last saw her parents, but she cannot find them.

That is how Hemingway ended up in the small village in the Andes. She needed to do something besides wake every day at 3:13 a.m. haunted by her parents' deaths. They died in a car crash the day after she graduated from college. Their present to her was a trip to Peru where she and her mother were scheduled to hike The Inca Trail. Hemingway ended up hiking it alone. Then she stayed.

She lived in a small village high in the mountains for a solid year. She became acquainted with each season intimately. Hemingway apprenticed with Cristina, a woman at the local weaving cooperative, where she learned how to weave and make dyes. She wandered mountain trails and collected herbs and flowers. She learned Quechua and lived by herself in a tiny cottage on the mountainside. She spent the year walking and weaving. She found herself again by taking the colored strands of yarn and making beautiful tapestries.

Every hour on the hour she heard the church bells chime in the village square, and learned to stop and listen. Cristina taught her to be still and pay homage to the bells. Often they were out gathering plants on the mountain side, and every time the bells rang, they stopped to pray and reflect.

Cristina taught Hemingway much more than how to weave and dye. She showed her how to be present in each moment. Hemingway learned to live with her deep grief about being an orphan.

At the end of the year, Hemingway returned to Savannah. She began going to BeeBee's Diner each morning for coffee and biscuits. She met Agnes, who became her surrogate mother. Agnes helped her accept that her days once again begin at 3:13 a.m.

Hemingway climbs out of bed and gets down on her knees and prays. She hears the barking dog outside her window and Cristina's voice in her head. Perhaps it is time for another visit to the Peruvian village high in the Andes Mountains.

For now, she will go to BeeBee's Diner and talk to Agnes.

Bavaria

Another Morning

The boy hurries along the cobblestone streets
Each morning he makes his way along these winding paths
For the prize he puts in his jacket close to his chest
A pound of bacon
He does not want to lose this special treat
That makes his taste buds sing
And his mother happy

He wants to please her
He likes her happy

Making his way in the dark is worth it
If he can only get past the man with the big dog
The boy does not know when he will appear
Each time he turns a corner the boy breathes a sigh of relief
His step is lighter
He is close to home now
Can it be true?
Is he safe this time?
He does not want to relax
Not yet

One more stretch of the narrow winding cobblestone street
He sees the light go on in Mr. Muller's house
He hears Dagna Webers' cough through her open window
Morning is coming
He sees Otto's red wooden flower box
Sun lighting wilting yellow daisies
That need water from the blue watering can

Does he dare stop and pour the precious liquid on the flowers?
Does he chance it?
Knowing it is possible he will not get home
Without meeting the man in the dark cloak
With his big dog who chomps at the bit
And pulls on the metal chain

Who is barely contained
Who wants the boy's bacon

Does he take the risk?
He must choose

The small beam of light on the daisies calls him
If they had only stayed in the shadows
He hears Mrs. Weber's tinkling voice
As she talks to her cat
He is later than usual
He knows these familiar sounds
People and their morning routines
The young woman at the window watches him
He looks up and nods
Their eyes meet
Shadows surround this dark haired beauty

He is distracted
The dog pounces
Nips the boy's hand
Sinks his teeth into the bacon
Stares at the boy as he pulls the meat from the boy's chest
The dog prances away
The boy stands watching his wagging tail
The young woman disappears
The man stands there
A witness to the boy's loss

His mother awaits him
He has no prize
Not today
The package is gone
The dog is fed

The boy picks up the blue watering can
And waters the flowers

Another day in this village has begun

So The Light Can Get In

My name is Sarja. I live in a cottage in the Black Forest. I am done with my chores for the day. I sit in stillness. The sun is out, but you wouldn't know it because the trees around my cottage are tall and dense. They block out the light. For as long as I can remember I have liked the dark. Yet today, as I sit quietly by the heat of the fire on this cool October morning, I want more light.

Fall is here. The days are getting shorter. It is the time of year when I usually go on retreat to a village in Spain or Portugal. This year, I need more light, so I am making my way to the Greek Island of Mykonos. I rented a white cottage with a blue door, that sits on the cliffs overlooking the blue water.

You would think that living alone at the end of a dirt path would be a retreat in and of itself, but I am not the only cottage-woods-dweller here. I visit my neighbor, Franz, once a month and have worn a path through the woods to his small cottage. Franz and I grew up in this forest, and when his father died, Franz asked me to help him clean out his father's house. I smudged the house inside and out with lavender and sage. Franz used stones to change the look of his place. I like the stones.

The other night my friend, Adele, the village post mistress, and I, sat by the fire at her place above the post office, sharing stories. We are the same age. She now yearns for the quiet of my cottage deep in the woods, and I want light and more connection with people. She is the one who first suggested I consider cutting down a ring of trees that surround my house. I sat in shock when she said that and immediately began arguing with her.

But when I left that night, I began to wonder if Adele might be right. As I walked with my small lantern through the darkness, before the full denseness of the woods overtook me, I turned around and looked back at all the shiny yellow glows in the village. I was clear-I needed more light. I wanted to see the sky-panorama of lights. Later that same week, I talked to Franz about wanting more light and the possibility of cutting down a ring of trees.

Seems to me it'll give you what you're looking for, he said.

I went back and forth about it. I live on Basha's Knoll, one of the few knolls in the area. If I cut down a ring of trees, I will have more light. For reasons unknown, I am tired of the dense darkness, and I am afraid to create more light because if I cut down the trees I will not be able to change it back. My little cottage will be exposed. People will be able to see me. I might feel too vulnerable, be too visible.

That's only from the air, Sarja, not from on the ground, Franz reminded me. He was right. I would only be more visible if someone walked down my path. To get to my place you have to go to the end of the main path, make a right and walk a quarter of a mile. We used to have a wooden sign with every woods-dweller's name on it. There is still a sign there, but the rain and snow have washed away the names. No one has replaced or repainted it, so now it's just a piece of weathered board. It is a marker though. When people come to visit for the first time, they can see where they need to turn. The path seems obvious to me because I have put stones along both sides of it.

The path is clear to you, Sarja, but not necessarily to anyone else, said Franz. He may be right. I don't really know. Hikers have wandered back here with their day packs. When they realize someone lives here they usually turn around and leave.

The next morning, I awoke with the dream of the sky opening up. I could see the stars at night and the sun during the day. That was the week a stranger knocked on my door. When I opened it, I was not happy. I gave him my strong silent look that said, *What the fuck are you doing here knocking on my door in the middle of a Wednesday afternoon?* He smiled at me and said, *I heard about you from Adele. She gave me directions to your place.* I found this hard to believe because Adele had never done this before, and she certainly wouldn't have done it without good reason.

He told me, *I'm Mikal. I just moved here. I talked to Adele at the post office while I was getting a P.O. Box and she told me you were thinking about cutting down some of your trees. I know how to do that.*

Now I understood why Adele sent him to me. Adele and I believe in synchronicity, that things happen just the way they are supposed to, that the universe lines things up to support intention. So, the tree-cutter arrived.

Mikal and I talked about trees and opening up space. He talked about first cutting down a small circle of trees to see if that

---

180

was enough light. *You could always widen the circle over time if and when you're ready for more light.* He drew it on paper so I could see exactly what he was talking about. His question was, *How exposed do you want to be?* I told him, *I didn't know, that I liked my privacy a lot, but lately I'd been wanting more connection with people.* He smiled and told me, *Trust your process.*

It has been three months since Mikal cut down the first ring of trees. Every day and night I bask in the new light. I do not understand the full extent of what is going on with me, but I am clear that I need more light. Mikal comes tomorrow to cut down the next circle of trees around my cottage. I trust my process. I honor my opening.

Sarja

In the beginning there is a woman and a man, the witch and the wanderer. The witch, Sarja, lives alone in a cottage deep in the Black Forest. The wanderer, Jakob, is passing through the small village on the day there is a village dance.

Jakob meets Sarja at the village dance. She is beautiful, mysterious, and alone. Jakob does not understand why she is alone because she is by far the most beautiful woman in the room. He can see that all the men are attracted to her, yet they keep their distance. During the break he asks one of the musicians why this woman is by herself.

Franz, the horn player, tells him, "Sarja has powers. She's a witch. She comes from a long line of witches."

The wanderer takes this in, but does not believe a word of it. He's a city boy, a vagabond of a sort, who's grown up to be a worldly, well-travelled man. Jakob cannot take his eyes off Sarja. She does the line dances and the men lightly hold her at the waist, barely grazing her fingers, as though somehow she will infect or electrocute them. The women eye her warily. The children love her, and although the parents have tried to keep their little ones from going to her, it does not work. The children gather round her, and she tells them stories. Their parents allow it because they do not want to scare their children, and they feel sorry for Sarja.

Sarja sees the wanderer staring at her and returns his stare. He cannot look away. The wanderer hears a little boy call to Sarja who turns to him with the biggest smile Jakob has ever seen. It is only when the little sprite of a boy runs and stands directly in front of Sarja that she stops staring at the wanderer. She turns her head and gives her full attention to the boy, who moves closer to Sarja and puts out his hands. She pulls him closer. He whispers in her ear. Sarja smiles. His mother watches them from the sidelines and is aware of her son's every move. When the music begins again, the boy lurches from Sarja's arms and runs to his mother.

Jakob goes to Sarja and holds out his hands just like the boy, arms outstretched, palms facing upwards. He wants her to take hold and pull him towards her like she did the small boy. Sarja looks at Jakob coolly and continues to observe him as he has been observing her. He is aware she is calculating, deciding. He doesn't think she's unsure. It looks to him like she's listening to a message no one else can hear.

When she takes his hands, he feels electricity shoot through him. He feels more alive than he can remember, perhaps more alive than he's ever been. Part of him wants to let go, yet she has a grip on him. It's not that she's holding on tightly because she's not. It is a larger gripping, a knowing that he must connect with this woman. He must see if she will dance with him.

Sarja and Jakob dance throughout the night. When she's not dancing she is telling stories to the children. Jakob stands at the edge of the story-circle, watching. He hears her words and her beautiful voice. She weaves a web that all the children want to be in. Her words calm them. Her stories paint a picture. The parents trust her and they fear her. She is a part of the village, a member of this community. Jakob is the outsider.

Jakob spends three days with Sarja. He doesn't know why she lets him in. At the time he doesn't care. He goes with the physicality and the sensuality. He goes with his lust and hers. He is surprised by her openness. She is hungry. He is too. He learns that most of the villagers do not really know her either, yet they accept her. Her family has deep roots here.

Sarja and Jakob speak of their dreams and desires. They walk in the forest. They make love under the dark trees. She wants him to be with her. She is willing. He wants to stay, but he cannot. It is Jakob who must move on. He tells her he would like to come back at a later time. She smiles a sad smile. She does not believe he will return. He argues weakly with her. He talks about work and other commitments. The truth is, he doesn't know if he will come back. In the end, this is what he tells her. She nods. She prefers the truth.

It takes everything he has to go. He doesn't know why he leaves.

Five years pass and he cannot stop thinking about Sarja. He doesn't know why he hasn't returned to the village. He thinks about writing to her. He thinks about just showing up in the village. He thinks about a lot of things, but he doesn't act. He has sex with women who mean nothing to him.

Jakob is at a crossroads. He needs to make a decision. Does he go to Sarja? Perhaps she is married. He doubts this, yet there is that possibility. He doesn't want to risk it. He's afraid he'll be disappointed, yet something keeps pulling him.

He talks to his friend and shop-mate, Jorgen, about his dilemma. Jorgen encourages him to go and tells him the shoe shop will be here when he returns. Jakob leaves with a small pack on his back filled with a change of clothes, a loaf of bread, and a large hunk of cheese. He wanders back to Sarja's village.

From a distance he watches a small blond girl with a knapsack come out of Sarja's cottage. She looks to be about five. He wonders whose child she is. Then he hears Sarja call to her. The small girl turns and calls her *Mama*. He is startled. The girl is the spitting image of him. The time line is right. He stands in the silence of the forest as the girl scurries off to school.

Long after the girl leaves, Jakob goes to the cottage door. Sarja is humming a haunting tune with notes in a minor key that seem to wander and stop in odd places. He listens to Sarja's sounds and the lyrics to her songs. She is telling stories to herself and to the walls of the small cottage. He is uncertain about what to do. Knock, don't knock. Walk in. Go away. He stands outside for a long time. Then he sits on the front stoop. Eventually Sarja comes outside and sees him. He looks at her. She eyes him warily at first. Perhaps she doesn't recognize him. Perhaps he's changed that much. She smiles that sad smile.

"You've come back?" There is a question and a statement that is held in these three words.

"Is she mine?" He asks.

"Yes. You're the only one."

"Why didn't you contact me?"

She says nothing. She looks at him coolly. It's an absurd question. It doesn't warrant a response.

"What's her name?"

"Anya."

"I like that name."

She smiles.

"Our daughter," she says.

His heart beats hard and loud. He wants this family. He wants this life. He wants to be a father and a husband. He wants it all. They move towards each other. She holds out her hands, palms upward. He remembers. He pulls her towards him. She opens her dress. He suckles her breast and smells her warm musty fragrance. He breathes her in. His need is strong. So is hers. They don't make it to the bed. They make love on the rug by the fireplace. She tells him afterwards she's pregnant again. He doesn't know how she knows this, but he knows she tells the truth.

He moves in that day. When Anya comes home from school, she tells him, "I told mama you were coming."

Viktor is born nine months later. He's the spitting image of Sarja.

Jakob sets up a shoe shop in the village. He sends a letter to Jorgen saying he won't be returning and asks Jorgen to take over that shop. The community happily takes Jakob in. His business thrives.

What matters to Jakob is Sarja and Anya and Viktor. Jakob doesn't know why it took him so long to return. Sarja assures him that he came at a perfect time, exactly when he was supposed to.

"There are no mistakes," she says.

He knows this is true.

The Button Pusher

I first see her in Vronsky's Curio Shoppe in a small village in Bavaria. I stop to look in the shop window, and there she is, standing at the counter with her spectacles on her nose. She appears to be examining something. I can't tell what. She must feel my eyes upon her because she glances up and sees me peeking in the window underneath Vronsky's. She holds my glance for a little longer than is socially acceptable, and I'm the one who turns away first, which is unusual for me. I'm usually the bold one, the one who people turn their heads to look at when I make an entrance. I enjoy being noticed. But with this woman, whose name I learn later is Magdalene, I wander away without going in.

I go to The Village Bakery and order a pastry and coffee. I sit quietly outside, reflecting on my attraction to Magdalene as I watch the villagers pass by. I am particularly drawn to a young couple who are exchanging harsh words. As the woman's voice gets louder, the man tries to comfort her, and she tells him loudly to stop trying to control her. After the waiter brings their coffee, the woman seems to calm down and the man moves, sits next to her, and rubs her back. The woman begins to silently cry. I turn my head away as this seems like a private moment that I have no right to be witnessing.

I'm uncomfortable. It's like I don't fit into my skin anymore. I don't know why. I don't have a history of being self-reflective, until now. I listen to people in the cafe chatting, but mostly I can't get Magdalene and the look we exchanged out of my mind. I can't stop my quickly beating heart and my palms getting sweaty.

Then I hear a woman at another table say something about Vronsky's.

"Have you seen the new buttons in Magdalene's shop? They're amazing! Carved and etched ivory."

As their conversation fades in and out, my mind begins racing. I wonder if Magdalene was looking at one of the new buttons before she saw me. I want to see those buttons. And who buys buttons these days, anyway? Then I start thinking about my gram's button collection and how she used to let me take out her buttons and look at them. When Gram got a new button, she would show it to me. There are women who are button collectors. My gram was one of them.

Suddenly I want to go to Vronsky's and look at Magdalene's buttons. I get up so quickly I nearly tip over the small table. I'm jittery from the coffee.

When I walk through the shop door, the bell jangles. Magdalene is talking with two women. She glances at me and nods. I nod back. Then she returns to her conversation that gets quieter, as though they don't want me to hear what they're saying.

After the women leave, I ask Magdalene about the new buttons. She's clearly surprised I know about them, and when I ask if I can see them, she shows me the buttons. They are works of art. Each one has a different, finely etched scene on it. I look at one of them with my magnifying glass and see a man on a corner handing a small package and money to another man. A woman is watching this exchange from behind a curtain. The button is telling a story. The attention to detail in each one of them is spectacular.

I tell Magdalene about Gram's button collection. Magdalene says that she comes from a long line of button collectors. I ask how much the buttons cost.

"They're not for sale right now," she says quietly. "There's a buyer for these particular buttons, but perhaps I can order you some different ones."

"Who's the artist?" I ask.

Magdalene ignores my question, and says, "I'm awaiting the arrival of the buyer of these buttons."

We lock eyes and some unspoken message is delivered.

"How about dinner tonight?" I ask her.

She tells me, "Unfortunately, I have plans. Can I take a raincheck?"

I nod, and she nods back. I put my card with my contact information on the counter.

When I go to Vronsky's a few days later, the shop's Closed sign is on the door.

The bust comes one week later.

The story in the paper reports that an anonymous tip led police to Vronsky's where they hoped to find Turkish hashish hidden in buttons. The curios remain, but Magdalene and her buttons are gone. They're calling her The Button Pusher.

187

I visualize the buttons and remember their unusual thickness. At the time I thought the thickness might make it easier for the artist to do the etching. I don't know if what the papers say is true, and I don't really care. I'm attracted to Magdalene. The truth is I have no idea who she is, but I'm pulled to find out.

Three weeks after the bust, I get a small note from Magdalene that says, *Meet me in Salzburg on 20 May if you so desire. Go to Platz Bruegel. You will find The Button Shoppe.*

I go. What do I have to lose?

When I walk in, Magdalene looks different. She has short coiffed blond hair and is wearing a tasteful green linen suit with stunning porcelain buttons. My heart starts pounding and my palms are sweating. She's sexy as hell. I want her. It's that simple. She looks at me, and I look at her. This time, I do not walk away. She's in business once again, and when she asks me to join her, I don't hesitate. These kinds of opportunities do not come along that often.

Coachella Valley

An Unwelcome Bargain

Admittedly I push you
And get more than I bargain for
You stand up
Look me directly in the eyes with a cold hard stare
Pick up your red leather purse from the floor
Pull your plum sweater from the back of the chair
I try to catch your eyes again
You are all business
You turn
I watch you walk away
You swish across the brown Mexican tiles
Your black and white pants show your gorgeous butt
You do not hurry
No one knows what happened
Just a woman going to the powder room
Soon to return

In the rhythmic measuring of your steps
I know you hold onto every ounce of control you have
I do too
I want to flip over the table
Scream at the waitress
Demand my check
Silence the noisy children whose parents are drinking too much
I do none of these

I sit quietly staring out the large window
I watch the waves gently and not so gently hitting the shore
They keep coming
Rolling in and rolling out
I hope you'll come back
I almost expect to see your face again
With your eyes now softened

The longer I sit
I know you are gone

You have walked away
I did not know at the time that it is for good

You change your phone number
I go by your small yellow wooden house with the red door
White flower boxes filled with petunias, poppies, and pansies
Three P flowers
I am shocked to see the FOR SALE sign
And the other sign that says OPEN HOUSE
A young couple laugh as they walk up the stone path
I sit in my car
Stuck
I cannot get out

I hear the voices of the realtor and the happy young couple
A bell rings
My throat tightens
How many times have I lain in your comfy bed
Wind blowing
Bells singing a chorus of rich notes
The high soprano
The tenor and the bass
Each one has their part
Their song indicates the kind of wind that blows
I know these sounds and tunes

You left your bells?

These treasures that you found
In an old shop in that small Italian village
We had been wandering all day
At dusk just before the sun went down
We happened upon a shop with a tiny sign in the window
CURIOS
Full of delights
The old man spoke good English
He told us he spent a year abroad studying Art History at Claremont

He loves Palm Springs

Yet this village is where he belongs
He returned home and is happy to be here

He flirted with you
And you with him
I did not feel threatened
I was amused
You worked your magic
It did not take him long to show you the bells
He had your number
And you his
He took you into a back courtyard where hundreds of hanging brass
bells sing
Your face beamed
Your blue eyes sparkled
Your laughter was wild and raucous
I don't know how you chose
He helped you
He knew how they worked
Soon you had your own little symphony
A pristine beauty of rich and haunting tones
You were entranced
I was stunned
He wrapped 13 bells individually in thick green paper
Put them in an old wooden box with a lid that had a brass clasp
He said he could ship them to you
But you would not let him
You could not let them out of your sight
You carried them on the train
You walked them onto the ship
You hung 3 of them by the window in our small stateroom
We were serenaded across the ocean
Everyone knew you as the bell lady

I am broken from my reverie by the young couples' laughter
They are exiting your sunny cottage
As I reach your green gate
They stop and listen to the bells
I hear them ask the agent if the bells come with the house

She says no
The bells are not for sale
The woman looks sad
The man wonders if the owner can be contacted
Perhaps negotiated with
The realtor shakes her head

No

Everything but the bells is negotiable
The man pushes and asks in a loud demanding voice
Can I speak with her?
She is gone
Unreachable says the realtor
I stop at the gate and listen intently to their conversation
The man's eyebrows arch
You can't get a hold of her?

No

The man persists
Why did the owner leave the bells?
The realtor sighs as she pushes her purple bifocals up on her nose
The owner feels the bells need to sing here just a little longer
They celebrate her upcoming departure

I am stunned by her response
It is so you
Your words

Then there is silence of a sort
The bells sing louder
Their haunting tones fill the air
This is your invitation says the agent with a slight smile and a
twinkle in her eye
The woman quietly nods and says
It is received

I know they will buy your house

I feel it as they walk away

It takes me a long time to step through your small green gate
I don't know what I'm doing
When the bells start again
All I can think of is you and me in bed together
Lollygagging that Sunday morning
Me in and out of you
You laughing and crying, parading around naked

As I make my way to your front door
I am lost in memories
I want to find out where you are
I do not believe you are unreachable
I do believe you do not want to be bothered

When I cross the threshold
I ask the realtor if I can wander around the house
Alone
She silently looks me over
I imagine she knows I will not buy
She may even know who I am
Maybe she hears my pain in the question
Or my hostility
She hears something
There is a moment of tension
Then the brown curly haired realtor nods

Yes

I don't know what I'm doing
I guess I want to see if I can feel you

The bells start again
I am sorry I pushed you
I got more than I bargained for

The Three-Year Birthday

Lexi looks across the terrace and sees two women in line, talking. The woman with her back to Lexi, dressed in lavender, is built like Evelyn. But lavender is not a color Evelyn ever wore. The other woman with long brown hair is in white linen, wearing heels, and has a big red purse. Lexi's eyes meet hers briefly, but there is no recognition. The woman is merely perusing the room, and Lexi must not seem interesting to her. Lexi sees the woman in white move slightly toward the lavender-dressed woman and push her hair off her face.

The intimacy of that gesture touches Lexi. She looks away. When she hears the woman in lavender's loud, raucous cackle, Lexi's heart begins to pound. It is Evelyn's laugh.

Gut-wrenching physical, emotional, and mental pain roar through Lexi like a tornado. She is in trouble. She texts Claire, her sponsor, and tells her, *Evelyn's here.* Claire texts her back. *Your birthday and Evelyn's leaving are triggers. Breathe. Order an Arnold Palmer. I'm on my way. Happy Birthday. Welcome to the never-ending gifts of recovery.*

Lexi sits with her pounding head in her hands. She keeps thinking, *this cannot be happening.*

"Ma'am?"

The waiter has come to the table where Lexi is sitting by herself. She hears concern in his voice.

"Ma'am," he says again, softly, but with a bit more urgency.

Lexi knows she should look up, but she doesn't know if she can. But of course she can, and she does. Briefly their eyes meet, and she sees caring in his rich, cocoa-colored eyes. She imagines he sees her pain and weariness, the kind that even if she slept a week, she would not be rested. She is like a thirsty person who cannot get enough to drink.

"Can I have a large Arnold Palmer with green tea?" Lexi asks.

The waiter nods.

What she could just as easily have said is, *bring me a margarita, double the tequila.* But she doesn't.

198

Today is Lexi's three-year clean and sober birthday and the fourth anniversary of Evelyn's leaving. After Evelyn left, it took Lexi a year to surface from the searing pain. Then she stopped all the alcohol and drugs. It wasn't easy, but somehow her desire to use was taken from her. Not that she didn't have passing thoughts of drinking and using, like today, a day of celebration and loss, polarities stuck together.

Before Evelyn walked out, they had been drinking too much. Lexi liked the hash better, but any mind-altering chemical would suffice. Evelyn was strictly alcohol, no drugs. She prided herself on this and had a lot of judgements about Lexi, who was an addict. Evelyn believed that people who used drugs were somehow different from, and less than, people who liked alcohol. Lexi tried to tell Evelyn that different chemicals worked for different people. Evelyn never bought it.

When Lexi looks up, she sees Claire and her friends. They are laughing and are trying to contain a big bouquet of colorful balloons. They call out, *Happy Birthday*. The waiter comes over and helps Lexi relocate to a table for ten.

Lexi sees Evelyn staring at her with a glass of red wine in her hand. Lexi looks right in her eyes, picks up her Arnold Palmer, and begins laughing and crying as her friends sing Happy Birthday.

The Wife

The wife stands at the bedroom window and cannot believe that her lover, Jordan, has stormed out. She doesn't want him gone, but he put the screws to her.

"Leave him or I leave you," said Jordan.

Cynthia did her cajoling, her pleading, and her sucking of his dick, just the way he liked it. He came into her from the back, and she was on fire. But in the end, the hot sex wasn't enough to keep him. She got parental, child-like, and finally she was an adult.

"I don't want you to go, Jordan. I love you."

Jordan broke in after her declaration, "Not enough to leave him, Cynthia."

It was true. She wasn't leaving Lewis. She wasn't. It had nothing to do with love. It had to do with lifestyle.

In her marriage Cynthia could mostly do whatever she pleased, and the money was virtually endless. She was careful, and had become more careful as the years went by. Lewis had always been generous financially. She wasn't on a budget exactly, but he was aware of how much money she spent. She didn't spend that much anymore. The clothes and the expensive lunches ended long ago. Once a month she made a trek to a small bank in Palm Springs to her safe deposit box, where she had over three million dollars. She knew exactly how much money she could take each month.

She only crossed the line once, and that was a long time ago. Lewis had been angry, but contained. It was when she was buying and using a lot of cocaine. He knew she was high and had told her he wasn't going to have it. He asked her to reign it in, and when she found she couldn't, she went to rehab and changed her life.

A couple of months later in one of her aftercare groups, she met Jordan and fell in love with him. She began her first and only sober affair.

Lewis knew Cynthia had a lover, but he didn't care about that, although he would have been surprised to learn that for the past twenty years, she had had only one lover. What Lewis liked was sex. Cynthia sucked his dick a couple of times a week and let him fuck her the other days. It was not about love for him. It was about release, getting off. Then Lewis was off to his day of meetings, managing his company and his money. Lewis liked the game and the big playing field.

After rehab, Cynthia tried to connect with her husband, but Lewis wasn't interested. He was glad she was clean and sober because she could show up at social events and act appropriately. This is what he cared about. They had no children. He had one adult son from a former marriage, and Cynthia liked Stephen, although Stephen stopped coming around about a year ago. Cynthia didn't know why. Lewis had taken him out of the will, and everything was going to Cynthia.

The other thing Lewis required, was that Cynthia be home in a reasonable amount of time after her AA meetings. He was fine with a social hour or so after the meetings, but then he wanted his wife home, to see her, talk to her, and have sex. This had been their routine for twenty years.

When Cynthia met Jordan, she was three months clean and sober. Jordan had a little over a year. The energy between them was electric. Cynthia's first sponsor directed her to not get involved with him. That lasted two months. After a meeting and coffee with a group of people, Jordan and Cynthia stayed at the restaurant and agreed to meet the next day for lunch at a little café in Silverlake.

Cynthia had her days to herself. Jordan was an artist, so Cynthia often went to his loft to read and write. The people in Jordan's apartment building thought they were a couple. The doorman, Fred, was a love. He had seen Cynthia's picture in the LA Time's Society Section, and knew her husband was Lewis Macabee, one of the wealthiest men in the world.

Fred was tight lipped. He played along with Jordan and Cynthia's game. Cynthia went by Amber in the other life she was living. At all her meetings she was known as Amber B., short for Amber Brown, a nice simple name. No problems. No attention drawn to her. But still, she was leading a double life, not the double life of chemical addiction, but a double life never-the-less. The wear and tear of that duplicity was beginning to take its toll on her. Writing about her life in a fictional context was no longer alleviating the pressure she felt from living these two lives.

When Jordan walked out, something broke inside of Cynthia. She had no interest in drinking and using, although, being an addict, it did cross her mind. She quickly ruled it out. What happened next was a surprise to her. Cynthia made a decision to move to Palm Springs and find a place that she could call home. She was sick of being Lewis Macabee's wife. She was sick of being Amber. She knew she was taking a big risk and once she left, she could never return to her old life. She packed a bag and took all her expensive jewelry. She didn't really need anything else. She left Lewis a note, thanking him for taking care of her financially all these years and told him she was leaving him. She made it clear that she would be filing for divorce, and that she had copies of all their assets. If he didn't want an ugly, messy, public divorce then splitting things fifty-fifty would be just fine. Cynthia had talked with an attorney years ago and had yearly meetings to make updates to her file, but she had not really planned on leaving Lewis then.

Jordan walking out on her today tripped a switch. She is ready to lead a different kind of recovery life. Cynthia doesn't know what her life will look like three months from now, but she is ready. She stands at the front door and looks around at the life she is leaving. It has been a life that is bittersweet. She has been taken care of financially and sexually, but emotionally, mentally, and spiritually, her life has been lacking. She wants more.

Tomorrow she will celebrate twenty-one years clean and sober in Palm Springs. She will go to the Wednesday 5:30 p.m. women's meeting and get her chip. She is ready to join this recovery community. What a birthday gift!

The Lottery Ticket

You and I buy a lottery ticket. We win ten thousand dollars! You take your half of the win and leave. I stand at the door screaming your name, asking why you're leaving. You never answer me. You never even turn around. I think you'll be gone a night or two or maybe a week. It never crosses my mind that it may be forever.

I know you wanted to visit your sick mother in Castine when she moved out of your childhood home into a skilled nursing facility. You believe she's dying. We have the same conversation over and over.

"Your mother blames me for taking you away, Jeremy, but you left on your own free will," I say.

"Mum doesn't see it that way. She believes I wouldn't have left if you hadn't come along."

"But that's not true," I object.

"Maybe, maybe not," you say.

"What does that mean?" I ask.

"I didn't have a strong urge to leave Castine. I liked it there. But you wanted to go."

"Really," I say. "That's not how I remember it."

You say nothing. Apparently you don't want any more conversation. So typical. I push you a little more, but you don't bite. It's a sore subject between us.

You stick to your story of leaving Castine because I am leaving. And the truth is—I was not staying in a town where I felt like I was dying. There was nothing there for me anymore. All my family died in that boating accident. Afterwards I lived alone in my family home until I met you, and we made a plan to move to Palm Springs. We! That's the key word here. You wanted to leave your mum who was suffocating you. You wanted to go 3500 miles. Did you forget that?

But you won't argue with me anymore. You're committed to buying one lottery ticket a week, and then we hit the jackpot, ten thousand dollars, five thousand each. In the scheme of things not that much, but enough for you to leave.

Three months after you leave I get an email from Maggie Teasdale telling me you returned to Castine, Jeremy. The prodigal son returns. I'm not surprised. I text you. You don't respond.

Maggie keeps in touch and tells me your mother died, and the whole town went to her funeral. She tells me you're back with your old girlfriend and she's pregnant. You said you didn't want kids, Jeremy. But now you're having one.

So, what was our seven years to you, Jeremy? Was I just a good fuck in the end and nothing more?

And now, on the year anniversary of our winning ten thousand dollars and your leaving, you send me one lottery ticket along with your marriage announcement.

Do I tell you I've won five point seven million and I'm not splitting it with you?

Cathy

The Room At The End Of The Hall

When I am five years old, my family moves from Minneapolis, Minnesota to Kirkwood, Missouri. My parents buy their first and only home, a small three bed room, one bath, wood and brick house. My bedroom is at the end of the hall. My mother puts colorful wooden letters on my bedroom door that spell *Cathy's Room*. Officially it is my room until I am eighteen years old and leave for Beloit College in Wisconsin. Sixty years later the faded letters of *Cathy's Room* are still on the door.

I love my childhood bedroom. I think it's the best room in the house. It gets a lot of light, and often there is a cross-breeze. It has two windows, one with a western exposure to the backyard, and the other, a northern exposure, with a side-view of the neighbor's white garage where I see different birds come and go. I don't hear or see the street. Not that there's a lot of noise, because it's a small circle street of twenty houses, one way in, one way out. We are house number five on the west side of the street. What I do hear and see are squirrels, sparrows, cardinals, and robins. My father has three bird feeders that he fills with different bird seeds so he can attract a variety of birds. I watch the birds from my bedroom windows. I love when the birds are migrating, and I get to see the yellow-breasted gold finches. The yellow is compelling. It draws me in every time.

When I look into the backyard I see apple and peach trees and a wooden fence with a wooden gate. When I pass through the gate I enter a magical world where I am greeted by a large weeping willow tree. As I walk further, I discover a hidden pond surrounded by trees and brush. This is a place where I can be myself and explore.

As a child and the only girl, my mother gives me her childhood maple bedroom set; a bed, dresser, and secretary. My parents transport her bedroom set from New York to Missouri when they buy their one and only home. The secretary is tall, with glass-paned windows that display books, art, and small sculptures. There is a pull-out desk that I open with an old key, that opens the glass cabinets as well. When I open the desk there are cubbies and a small drawer where I can put things. I hide things here, too. When I go looking for something and end up finding a long-forgotten treasure, I experience a kind of magic.

I am twelve the first time my mother and I redecorate my room. We strip the three pieces of maple furniture and paint them antique green. My mother and I work together in the one-car garage with the door open. There are numerous small tins and brushes which we use in a certain order. My mother is in charge of the order, and I follow her directions. We laugh, talk, and sing along with the music. We have fun! After we finish painting the furniture, I choose a new green and white pin-striped bedspread and curtains that match the newly-painted furniture. I love doing this project with my mother. I love that she gives me the freedom to pick the paint and the linens.

Years later when I get home from camp my mother surprises me by redecorating my room, again. She picks a yellow-orange bedspread with multi-colored stripes on the sides with matching curtains and paints the room a soft yellow. Later she tells me she was nervous about making these changes. She was scared I wouldn't like them.

Today, I admire her for taking that risk. And yes! I love that she painted my room yellow and picked bright colorful new linens. My mother and I share the love of color.

After I leave for college, my mother uses my room for her clothes and some of her personal items. Once again she strips the green secretary. This time she paints it fire-engine red and moves it to the basement. Later she transforms all three pieces of the bedroom set back to the original maple. She brings the secretary back upstairs and puts it into my bedroom.

My mother and I were not close, yet I see how she tried to make inroads into the difficult terrain of our relationship. When my mother gave birth to me, my parents realized they needed help. My mother called her mother who refused to come help her. My father then contacted his mother who came and took care of my mother and me. My mother felt beholden to her mother-in-law her entire life. My mother usually had a lot of confidence and was able to tackle most things with a lot of success; her athletic endeavors, running the Girls' Athletic Club, and starting a nursery school in Kirkwood are just a few of her accomplishments. The challenge of being a mother to a daughter who adored her father, even though she spent long days with me, did not feel good to her. Her time was no longer her own. The adjustment was difficult.

My mother told me it was not easy to have a daughter who did not look anything like her. I had straight blond hair and blue eyes like my father. She had brown curly hair and brown eyes. When I was little, people were always asking her if she was the baby-sitter. She told me this made her mad. I know she struggled being a young mother, as she was an only child and had no idea how to take care of a baby. She had no idea how to nurture anyone. Her mother was unable to teach her this.

It took me a long time to have compassion for my mother. I am grateful to remember the good times my mother and I had working on my bedroom together. I am grateful to have had a conversation with my mother about how distant she held me in all my baby pictures. My interpretation was that she did not love me. She told me she did love me and that she was scared. I believed her. Our last conversation was about my weight. When my partner said, *Cathy always thinks she's too fat*, my mother turned to me and said, *you're perfect*. I told her I loved her and said good-bye. These were the last words my mother and I said to each other.

After she died I cleaned out the secretary and found her hidden treasures in the cubbies. She had my Girl Scout badges in a wooden box, a bunch of letters wrapped with a blue rubber band that I wrote her from camp, Istanbul, and California, and a lock of my blond hair from my first haircut tied with a yellow ribbon.

I see how my mother tried to connect with me. She loved me the best she could. I am sorry we were not closer.

At The Dinner Table

My mother's voice rings like a church bell
Right on time
Every night at 5:30
Dad wanders in from the living room where he's been reading the
paper or watching the news
My brother explodes out of his bedroom where he's been doing God
knows what
No doubt he's hungry
I quietly emerge from my bedroom at the end of the hall and walk
towards the kitchen
It's surprising we never have a traffic jam or a collision
I always know the call's coming
Because earlier I get the 3 sharp knocks on my closed bedroom door
My summons to set the table with the melamine dishes that my
mother bought with her books of green stamps
Four colors: yellow, green, blue, pink
I always give myself the yellow plate
The others I mix up
Green could work for me
Never blue or pink
Color has always mattered
What if I'd ended up with pink? Or blue?
I wouldn't have eaten
I couldn't have
A hunger strike
Possibly a broken plate
Except melamine doesn't break easily
I would have had to smash it purposefully
And that would have changed everything for one night at the dinner
table
I would have liked that

Cathy's Journey

When I was eighteen years old, I left Kirkwood, Missouri and went to Beloit College in Wisconsin. Unbeknownst to me, I started a journey to find and recover myself. It was 1969 and the war in Vietnam was in full swing. Even though I was dissatisfied with western culture, I applied for foreign study in London and Copenhagen. My college advisor understood my dissatisfaction and talked about immersing myself in a completely different culture in a third world country. He suggested that I consider studying in Istanbul, Turkey. I was open to his suggestion. I applied and got accepted at Robert College, a small American school in Bebek, a suburb of Istanbul.

My parents came to Beloit for a weekend and we discussed my choices with the Foreign Study Director. In that discussion my parents expressed concern about my use of marijuana. The Foreign Study Director talked about how experimentation with drugs and alcohol is often a part of a college student's individuation process. He didn't believe I had a problem.

The most memorable part of that meeting was my father saying, *If you go to Turkey, I'll disown you.* My immediate response was, *Dad, I'm going to Turkey.* He could have stopped me from going overseas because he paid my tuition, but he didn't. I felt triumphant.

When it was time to go to Istanbul my father and I cried and clung to each other with unexpressed hurt and anger. Both of us felt the threat of abandonment. My mother stood silent. As I walked down the ramp, I felt wrenching sadness and deep grief.

I was nineteen years old when I arrived in Turkey with one suitcase and a small carry-on bag. Those were the days of travelling light. When I stepped off the plane I was immediately aware of how different Turkish is from English. Most people there did not speak English. I stood alone, waiting for my luggage that never came. As I considered what to do, a handsome, curly-haired young man came up to me and told me he was there to pick me up. I breathed a sigh of relief as Nico talked with the airport officials about my lost bag. I was upset and grateful that Nico found out my luggage was left in

London and would be delivered the next day. Nico and I got into a taxi that weaved through Istanbul to Robert College.

The next day Nico accompanied me back to the airport to get the suitcase that my parents bought me for this journey. It was the ease and acceptance that I am most aware of-luggage lost, a brief period of upset, acceptance, luggage found. I was grateful for Nico's help in retrieving the suitcase, and began to settle into my new life.

The courses at Robert College were taught in English; however, the students spoke Turkish in the dorms. I was assigned a top bunk where I watched the girls laugh and chat with each other. I had no privacy. I was alone in a sea where I had not yet found my mooring.

I left behind many remnants of home and plunged into a middle-eastern culture that I knew nothing about. I left the familiarity of what I knew and ventured to a place where I must learn my way. I was not afraid to wander and not know where I would end up. I discovered that I was an experiencer and an adventurer. I was a gypsy.

Movement was something I had always relied on. I ran around the college campus, but quickly learned that Turkish girls did not work out in public except when they were on a sports' team. I stopped running. I wanted to blend in as much as possible. I took up long-distance walking and explored Istanbul on foot. I was always looking, seeing, experiencing. I wove my way down the sidewalks to avoid Turkish men who wanted to physically run into me, a blond, blue-eyed American girl. I was lonely and movement was my way of coping with my loneliness.

When I stopped running, I gave up my primary coping mechanism. I missed the track at Beloit College. I ran there every day and it assuaged my loneliness. Now I was in Turkey at a college overlooking the Bosphorus, and I could not run.

Then I found a new coping mechanism, Turkish hashish in golden brown sticks. After my morning classes, Jo, the only other American girl on campus, and I, went to her friend Richard's apartment. We talked and laughed. I am glad I had a place to go where people spoke English. We got high and ate candy corn that Richard got from the commissary on base. I loved the white, orange, and yellow candy. I could not get enough of it. Over the next few months I gained forty pounds by eating candy corn and the rich baked goods that I consumed at the weekly three-hour seminar for foreign exchange students. Eventually smoking hash had nothing to do with my friends. The drug became my friend. It was the drug that I could depend on. It was the drug that changed my life.

I left campus most afternoons and wandered all over Istanbul by myself, breathing in Turkish culture, walking the downtown streets. I could not blend in. I went to B-rated American movies to hear English and feel the momentary comfort of home. I loved Turkish food. I found the best place for doner (lamb) sandwiches, yogurt kabobs, and baklava. I ate fresh cucumbers that I got from a vendor with his big wooden wagon. I loved the fresh fruit and vegetables and the thick, tart, bottled apricot juice. I loved the lamb cooking on the spit. I bought simits, which are similar to bagels, and smothered them with apricot jam. The tastes of all the foods were fresh and strong. My palate was satisfied.

I loved the friendliness of the Turkish people. They might not like America, but I never felt they did not like me. I chose to stay in Istanbul a second year. I taught English at a Turk-American Cultural Association. My students were adults who spoke Turkish and French and now needed English, the current international language, to succeed in their careers. They read a play about Darwin. I loved that my students worked at expressing themselves in English on the difficult subject of creationism. These discussions made me feel alive and reminded me of my father, who was working on a book about the Darwin family. I missed my dad. I smoked hash and ate candy corn. There was never enough of either of them to fill the hole in my heart.

I got a Turkish lover, Samim, and after three months we decided to live together. We found a small one-room apartment that usually served as the maid's quarters for the apartment complex. It had a cook-top, small fridge, and bunk beds. We took it over from two American women who were returning to California. We were lucky to get it. We had to lie and say we were married.

I bought birth control over the counter at the local drug store. No questions asked.

There is something about having sex and then sleeping separately that makes me wonder if this affected my future intimate relationships. I see how I can only tolerate a certain amount of intimacy and always crave space. More likely, the truth is, I already had intimacy issues long before I ever had a lover. Sleeping alone and waking up in my own space works for me. It goes along with being the lone walker, movie-goer, and traveler.

I woke every morning to the cacophony of children's voices speaking Turkish, German, French, Arabic, English and other unidentifiable languages. I found this comforting. I bought strong, thick, tart yogurt from a man who wandered around the apartment complex carrying yogurt in two metal discs that he balanced with a wooden bar that sat across his shoulders and upper back. During Ramadan I watched the apartment owners cut the neck of a lamb and give the meat to those who were less fortunate. I learned to drink strong espresso in tiny cups. I loved the strong rich taste. I was home in Turkey.

After twenty months I left Istanbul and returned to America to finish my degree at Beloit College. I found the readjustment to living in the United States difficult. Before returning to college I visited my parents and felt pulled into the old family patterns. I did not want to lose my newly discovered self.

When I returned to Beloit I could not find hash. I began smoking marijuana. Although it was not as strong as the hash, it gave me the feeling I wanted. I began smoking daily.

When I graduated from college, I got a job teaching outdoor education in western Massachusetts. At night, after the kids went to bed, I wandered outside by myself and sat in the snowy woods and smoked. I discovered I did not want to live in a place with cold winters, so after a year I packed all my possessions into my two-tone blue '68 VW Bug and headed west. I stopped in St. Louis for a brief visit with my parents and then headed to California. I hung my leather gypsy-girl that I bought in Turkey from my car mirror. My metal Nancy Drew lunch box filled with marijuana sat in the passenger seat. My books, papers, and typewriter that I depended on for comfort and solace filled the backseat. Did I need to go 3500 miles to California? Apparently I did. I required a lot of space to not lose myself, to continue finding myself, and to hear my voice.

I used marijuana and sex to soothe my loneliness. They worked, until they didn't. At some point no amount of books, movement, drugs, and sweets could mask my desperate loneliness and the addiction that claimed me. I felt powerless and my life was unmanageable. I could not figure out how to reconcile my addiction with my primary values of self-sufficiency and independence. I could not stop using drugs on my own. Humility came slowly, slowly, and then I stopped struggling. I had a breakthrough. I got into recovery.

I continued to move from place to place. The wandering gypsy did not die easily. It took years of moving around for me to find a physical home. Finally, after twenty-nine years of being clean and sober, a successful career, a partner of twenty-five years and the raising of three children, I got stopped in my tracks. Home found me!

Now I live in the Coachella Valley where I walk the desert trails in the canyons and the mountains. I still wander, but not the way I used to. I find myself gradually expanding my definition of home. I now know that home is internal and that to actually find a physical place that I call home is an amazing gift. I have put down roots in the desert. The starkness of the grey mountains and the desert's vibrant spring colors have captured my heart.

I am the swaying orange ocotillo blooms and the pink barrel cactus flowers. I am the green rose-breasted hummingbird who twitters and rests in her new nest. I am the settled gypsy with a colorful open heart.

Glass Beads

As my mother's Alzheimers progresses, I ask my father, "Can I have Mom's glass-bead necklace?"

His immediate reply is, "No!"

No hedging. No hesitancy. Simple clarity. Unusual for my wordy father.

He says, "After your mother and I returned from New Zealand, we took a bead-making class. We each made ten beads."

When I question him about some of the individual beads, he says, "Your mother wanted to make a necklace with the beads. I thought that was a great idea. We sat at the kitchen table together and I watched her move the beads around on a white flannel pillowcase. When she felt she had a good arrangement she asked me what I thought. I had no complaints about the lay-out. She always had a good eye for that kind of thing."

"So you don't know which beads you made?" I ask.

"No. I don't." My father is quiet. Then he says, "I used to know, but once we made a decision to combine our beads, that wasn't important to me anymore. What mattered was how beautiful your mother looked when she wore the beads."

I am touched by my parents' collaboration around the making of that necklace. My mother wore it for over twenty years. It was her favorite piece of jewelry. She had lots of expensive jewelry that my father bought her, but none of those pieces captured the essence of her and their relationship like that beaded necklace. Their love, connection, and melding of their lives was held by each colorful, unique, chunky, lop-sided bead.

I am surprised by my father's collaboration story. I have been raised to be fiercely independent and collaborating has been challenging for me. I have difficulty negotiating those waters.

When my mother falls and breaks her hip, she goes into rehab. My father begins to come to grips with not being able to take care of her at home any longer. After rehab she goes to an Alzheimer's Unit. He visits her at the care home at least once, and often twice a day. His love for her is strong. He misses her and how their relationship has been. He is losing his best friend. He cries a lot. Her transfer to the Alzheimer's Unit is like the nail in a coffin.

He lives alone for the first time in sixty-three years. He is lonely. His denial about her getting better cracks. He is heart-broken.

Every day my father looks at my mother's glass bead necklace hanging from the jewelry-tree on her dresser. When she dies on Christmas Eve 2011, my father's birthday, my father gives me the glass-bead necklace.

He tells me, "Your mother would be so happy to see you wearing her beads. I miss her so much. I don't have a clue how I'm going to live without her."

We cry together.

Today I proudly wear the gift of my parents' joint collaboration around my neck. Their relationship is a testament to love, dedication, and commitment. The glass bead necklace reminds me of the preciousness and power of love.

Today Is The Day

Today is the day I stop pretending
tell myself I want to at least

Today is the day I stop lying
know I need to
I keep hearing The Voice say
trying is lying

Today is the day I stop trying
I will or I won't
When I do, I do
When I don't, I don't

Today is the day I join the ranks of the committed ones

Today is the day I look myself in the mirror
and see who I really am

Today is the day I let go of all the pretenses
and all my old stories

Today is the day I stand tall, naked
I see who I have become

Today is the day I shake myself dry
I see words swimming in water on the floor in tiny puddles

Today is the day I actually look at these words
I begin to make sentences

Today is the day I create paragraphs from the small pools of words

Today is the day I fall in love with myself as Writer

Today is the day I stop making excuses
I set my intentions

Today is the day I begin my next book

Today is the day I find myself swimming in a Sea of Words

Today is the day I am finally home

The Metamorphosis

A metamorphosis is a remarkable change. My life has had a number of extraordinary changes. On 1 August 2011 after I said my good-byes and honored my co-workers with individual home-made cards and a copy of my CD, *The Year The Muse Came and I Listened*, I left the County Crisis Unit for the last time. I cried. I also felt incredible relief and excitement. My retirement had begun!

The next morning before we left our home in Napa, California, I declared, *I am going to change my life.* Then my wife, Lori, my son, Emmett, and I headed cross country to Maine with our mantra for the day, *Get out of California.* And we did. We got to State Line, Nevada that first night and celebrated with a swim in the lake and a wonderful Brandi Carlile concert. The old adage is, *You take yourself with you wherever you go.* I know this is true. I also know now, nearly three years later, that what got set in motion with that declaration was a transformation so great that I could never have believed or imagined how my life would change.

I worked from 16 to 60 years old. Lori and I had been together for 22 years. We raised three children. We bought and sold three family homes in Napa, and purchased a funky, 485 square foot cabin on a lake in south central Maine, for pleasure and as a personal retreat.

For eight years that cabin has been a haven, a nest, a quiet, simple space to sit and watch osprey, eagles, loons, great blue herons, and migrating Canadian geese. We kayak, swim, and hike there, too. I carry buckets of water from the lake to the porch, so we have water for flushing the toilet and washing the dishes. We get drinking water once or twice a week from a spring where we fill twenty, one-gallon jugs. We have no running water or shower at the camp. We heat water and pour it over each other to bathe. That ruggedness is juxtaposed with a Tempur-pedic bed, red comfy microfiber couches, and colorful, stained glass pole lamps from LL Bean.

Often things are not as they appear. Stories are more complicated than they may seem at first. Our cabin was, and still is, a place to leave all the stress, strain, and needs of other people behind. We unwind, relax, go inward, and be creative. It is a place where I get to hear the calls of the loons and decipher their conversations at midnight or 3:13 in the morning when I wake up to go to the bathroom or to write. I don't have to worry about time, even though sometimes I still do.

My spirit thrives here. Our cabin in Maine is a place that honors and waits for the creative self to show up. After the busyness and noise of normal life, our cabin provides a place of respite, a home for *The Self* to flourish. I put pen to blank paper and write, and pick up a paint brush and paint pictures I love. I am a writer though, so the words and the blank page are more often what call me.

It is not just one thing that brings forth a remarkable change. It is a series of events, people, places, and situations. It is an increasing ability to work with my thoughts, and be open to, and accepting of, impermanence and change.

In my 2009-2010 Animus Valley Institute Soul Year I experienced the force and the flow of a change-process, a major transformation, where I declared, *I am Water Carrier*. That claiming came directly from The Muse who visited me regularly that year. When I woke at 3:13 a.m. I heard words running through my mind. Only once did I not respond. I was tired and did not want to get out of bed. That morning The Muse gave me this poem.

It is like this
When she wakes in the morning darkness early
Before even the first signs of life
Before dawn has shown her pretty little head
This woman who comes every morning
With new possibility
With hopes for this new day
With treasures in store
If you are only open to receiving them
Do your part
Respond to the call whatever time it comes
You do not get to pick when The Muse comes for a visit
She comes when she feels like it
This time the words are 1-2-3, connect the dots
That's what you get
And you can go with it or not
She waits to see what you will do

She doesn't care if you're tired
She wants to know if you have what it takes to follow the thread
To see where it goes without judging if something is good or not
Because it does not matter
What matters is the response to the call
Prostrating yourself to the words
Committing yourself to the process, the not knowing
Yet trusting that something will come
That you will be rewarded
And the world will be better for it.

That morning I learned that I will always respond to The Muse's call, that She is a treasured gift. And then I heard myself say, *I am Writer and Storyteller*. At first I was shocked. How could I be so ballsy? I write. Yes! I have written for as long as I can remember. But to say, *I am Writer and Storyteller*. That bold claiming took my breath away, got my juices flowing, made me nervous, and evoked a fear so big that I imagined being struck by a lightning bolt. I felt not only a tremendous sense of responsibility to be Writer and Storyteller, but an overwhelming gratitude for being given this gift. I could no longer hide in the wings. I needed to express my voice and tell my stories for the benefit of the human race.

Soon after I claimed myself as Writer, Storyteller, and Water Carrier, *I found my home*, that still place inside me, that unbeknownst to me, I had been looking for all these years. I also found my physical home in the Coachella Valley, first in La Quinta, and then in Palm Springs.

We closed down our northern California storage unit after twenty months and brought everything by U-Haul to the southern California desert. We got rid of almost everything. I kept my books, my two green steamer trunks full of journals and other writings, and a large wooden table that now serves as my writing desk. I got my studio, *A Room of One's Own* as Virginia Woolf writes about in her book with this title. I transformed my room with wall to wall bookcases. I included my mother's old German wooden figurines that sat in her childhood room, then in mine. These 'little treasure people' are about an inch tall, painted in bright colors, and are at a celebration. There is a cake-holder, a woman holding a fire-cracker, a man playing an accordion, a woman dancing, and two milk maids.

They remind me of the importance of history and rootedness, and of the value of celebration and community. As Simone Weil says, *To be rooted is perhaps the most important and least recognized need of the human soul.*

Today in Palm Springs, I am Writer, Storyteller, and Water Carrier. I have a room with a view of the San Jacinto Mountains. I have the best wife I could ever hope to have, and the greatest life I could ever want. I have friends. I am part of the Coachella Valley community. My life keeps changing, and I keep showing up, open and willing. I cry when I leave home for a day, a night, a week, or the summer. I do not know why. I do know that I always cried when I left my childhood home in St. Louis and I never cried when I left Napa.

Every time I return home now, I feel joy. The love I feel for my desert home keeps growing. I have found my internal and external home. I am full of gratitude.

My soul sings.

Acknowledgments

I have many thank you's and deep appreciation and gratitude for all the help and care that I have been graced with throughout this book process-a birthing.

To Lee, my writing partner-For showing up every Wednesday to write and read our stories. Telling the truth. You gave me tough love and taught me how to edit.

To Robin, my daughter, not by birth, but by choice-For your dedication, many skill sets, and honesty. I couldn't have birthed this project without you.

To Lori, my partner of 28 years-For time and space, support, loving honesty, and clawing our way to grace.

To Lara Tupper, my original editor-For your attention to detail, honest feedback, and positivity. You believed in me! Your encouragement helped me move my book forward.

To my AVI Soul Group-For your listening, feedback, and sharing yourselves with me. You helped me claim I am Writer and Storyteller.

To my Covina Imagery Group-For love, listening, and generosity of spirit. Nothing better than journeying together and sharing!

To Grace, Helen, and Jane, my PW buddies-For sharing writes every week and taking the risk of excavating my life. I am a better writer because of you.

To Maura and Wendy, my hiking trio-For listening to many drafts of my stories and liking my writing. Walking these desert trails and canyons together provided inspiration for my stories.

To Katya-For generous listening and honest feedback.

To Ristretto staff—For great coffee and abundant space every Wednesday.

To Emmett, my son-For being a loving person with fierce determination and strong moral character.

To Heather, my other daughter-For love, support and being a great mother to Maxx and Mya, two beautiful young souls.

To my mother and father-For being role models for focus and persistence.

And last, but not least, to My Muse, who woke me many mornings at 3:13 with words to put on the blank page. And I listened.